NAIROBI
NIGHTMARE

By W. A. Sorrells

Illustrations by
Tom Bancroft and Rob Corley

Published by KidsGive, LLC
5757 W. Century Blvd., Suite 800, Box 8
Los Angeles, California 90045

Karito Kids™ and KidsGive™ are trademarks of KidsGive, LLC.

Cover art by Funny Pages Productions, LLC (Tom Bancroft,
Rob Corley, and Jon Conkling)
Interior illustrations by Funny Pages Productions, LLC
(Tom Bancroft and Rob Corley)
Journal created by Wendy Tigerman
Interior design by Andrea Reider, Reider Publishing Services
Manuscript consulting by Shoreline Publishing Group LLC

ISBN-13: 979-0-9792912-1-0

Printed in China. First printing, 2007.

Visit Karito Kids at karitokids.com.

The first books in the series of Karito Kids™ Adventures are dedicated to Steve and Jeff for their constant support and belief in KidsGive; Hannah and Will for their enthusiasm for KidsGive's goal of helping children around the world; Dave for his commitment and friendship; Andrea for her awesome work and dedication; Janet for her humor and belief in us; and last, but most certainly not least, Julie for her spirit and chutzpah. We couldn't have done it without you. Thank you for helping us imagine, create, and become.

—Love, Laura and Lisa

Your Code Number is 895572001063.

MORE THAN JUST A BOOK
Find Out All The Ways To Enjoy This Mystery Adventure

Each Karito Kids™ Adventure is much more than simply a book. By reading this book and visiting karitokids.com, you can explore countries, solve mysteries, and best of all help kids in need in other parts of the world. Get to know all the Karito Kids and become a part of an exciting new community of kids who care!

1. **Activate Your Charitable Donation**. If you purchased this book with a Karito Kids Doll, you may have already activated your donation. If you purchased this book by itself, go to karitokids.com and follow the online instructions to activate your donation. Three percent of the price of this book will be donated by KidsGive on your behalf to the children's charity Plan. The best part is that you will get to choose the cause to which you want your donation to go. You decide how you want to make a difference!

2. **Go to karitokids.com.** Check out our Karito Kids Book Blog where you can learn more about your favorite characters, where they live, and other fun stuff. You can even share what you think about each adventure, the actions they took, and the choices they made. You can find out what other kids think, too!

3. **Look For Culture Crossings**. While you're reading this story, keep your eyes open for places in the book where another country or culture is mentioned. Located within the story, illustrations, or journal, these places are called "Culture Crossings." When you locate a place in the book where another country (other than the country the story is about) is mentioned, go to karitokids. com and visit the "Culture Crossings" area and follow the online instructions. As with all Karito Kids games, you will also earn virtual *World Change* that can be accumulated and then donated by KidsGive on your behalf (as real money) to Plan. You might also find a few surprises!

4. **Solve Hidden Quests**. Each Karito Kid has so many adventures to share. Log onto karitokids.com and visit the "Hidden Quest" area to join her on additional quests. Just as with "Culture Crossings," you can earn virtual *World Change* that can be accumulated and donated by KidsGive on your behalf (as real money) to Plan.

Join up with other kids who are *Playing for World Change!*_{sm}

WHAT IS KARITO KIDS™ ALL ABOUT?

We launched Karito Kids™ to help connect children around the world in a number of ways.

- The word "Karito" means charity and love of one's neighbor in the constructed language Esperanto. We hope that children around the world strengthen their connection with each other, creating a global village of peace and understanding.
- Each Karito Kids Doll helps children recognize and appreciate the beauty of the world's many different ethnicities.
- The book that accompanies each Karito Kid tells a fun story involving that girl. It brings to life another country and its culture and connects readers to the notion that children from across the world have many fundamental similarities.
- The unique online activation process will allow children to directly participate in giving. They can determine the cause to which they wish to direct a percentage of the purchase price of the product. They can receive updates on the project they choose and find out how they helped children somewhere else in the world.
- Combining traditional play with innovative interactive games provides your child a play date with kids all over the world. They will have the opportunity to write to children sponsored by KidsGive and learn how children live in other parts of the world.
- Our selected charity, Plan, is a non-profit organization that is bringing hope and help to more than 10 million children and their families in poor communities worldwide. KidsGive contributes 3% of the retail price to one charity to maximize the impact of change.

~~~

m o j a

*L*ulu! Lulu! Lulu!"

The crowd of fifty thousand fans at Nairobi Stadium is on their feet, chanting my name. "Lulu! Lulu! Lulu!"

Team Kenya is tied with Team USA in the final game of the Women's World Cup. Forty-one seconds to go. My teammate Amina passes me the ball at midfield. There are three defenders between me and the goal. The odds are not good. Where are my teammates? It looks like I'm going to have to do it all myself. I do my patented stutter-step fake, then cut sharply to the right, beating my opponent at midfield and heading straight for the goal.

One of the defenders charges me—a girl twice my size, her forehead furrowed with determination. I sidestep her as she thunders past, breathing like a wildebeest. She's too slow to catch me!

"Lulu! Lulu! Lulu!"

Thirty yards out. Only Team USA's best fullback and the number-one female goalie in the world stand between me and victory. It's now or never! I pull my foot back to take the most powerful shot of my life and. . . .

"Lulu!"

It was my mother calling me. I blinked under the bright studio lights that surrounded us. We were in the middle of shooting *KenyaKidz*, the children's TV program my mother hosts.

"Lulu!" Mama said sharply. "Come back from Lulu Land!"

I blushed. I have a tendency to float off into a daydream world that Mama calls Lulu Land.

"Do you have a question for Mr. Garama?" Mama asked.

Ruta Garama, the best-known sculptor in Kenya and the special guest on her show, stood smiling at me. Waiting for me.

I've been a cast member on *KenyaKidz* since I was about eight years old. But I still forget my lines sometimes. I stared at Mr. Garama. Then I looked at the sculpture he had brought from the National Museum. There, on top of a white pedestal in the middle of the studio, stood a

sculpture of a man with piercing eyes and a long spear in his hand.

The sculpture was a model Mr. Garama made for a much larger sculpture that sits in front of Parliament House, Kenya's most important government building. It represents a Mau Mau, one of the soldiers who fought for Kenya's independence.

I gulped. My heart was beating like crazy. I had absolutely no idea what I was supposed to say. Truthfully? My mind was still back in the football game. Football is pretty much the only thing I think about these days. (Some people in North America call football "soccer.")

Mr. Garama was looking at me. His crazy-looking sculpture stared at me with its wild, accusing eyes. My mama stared at me. The director and the cameramen stared at me. The other kids on the show stared at me. In fact, since we were shooting the show live, half the kids in Kenya were staring at me.

"Uhhhhh . . ." I said. I wanted to crawl under my chair and die!

In the video monitor I could see myself. I'm a slim girl with dark brown eyes and brown skin that people tell me is a beautiful rich color. My black hair hangs down to my shoulders. And right now my eyes were as big as pie plates. In fact, I was completely frozen!

Suddenly everything went black.

And when I say everything went black, I don't mean it got dim. I mean *black*. TV studios have no windows. There were no lights at all. It took me a moment to realize that the power had gone out.

There were a couple of muffled thumps, then people started asking, "What's going on? Where's the light?" and things like that. People began moving around, bumping into things.

Then I heard my mother's voice. "Stay in your places! Don't move! Stay in your places!

Keep quiet. The generator will come on in just a moment and we'll continue broadcasting!"

It was dead silent for a little while. Then I heard another thump and some footsteps. I wondered who was walking around on the set. Then there was a crinkling noise, like someone wadding up heavy paper.

A few seconds later, the lights came on. Everyone blinked and squinted under the ring of powerful studio lights. Until our eyes adjusted, it was like staring at the middle of the sun.

My mother smiled. "Well, we're back!" she said brightly to the camera. "We had a few technical difficulties there, but now we've got them sorted out. Before the break we were asking Lulu what she thought of. . . . "

And then she stopped and stared. All our eyes turned to where she was looking. There, in the middle of the studio, was the white pedestal. With nothing on it.

"My sculpture!" Mr. Garama gasped. "My sculpture is gone!"

mbili

There was a long, terrible silence.

Then Mukanda the World's Funniest Clown came out of the darkness, doing backflips all the way, and landed on top of the pedestal. He struck a pose with a stern look on his face. He looked just like the sculpture.

"I'm back!" he said. "Aren't I a lovely sculpture?"

Mama smiled weakly. "Oh, Mukanda!" she said. "You're playing another one of your jokes, aren't you?"

Mukanda's eyes opened comically and his mouth gaped wide. "A *joke*? Me?" He struck another pose.

Everyone laughed.

The show was almost over. Mama made a few more remarks, then wound up the show.

As soon as the studio went out, the famous sculptor turned to her and asked, "What happened to my sculpture?"

"Mukanda!" Mama called. "Where did you put the sculpture?"

Mukanda was on the other side of the room, removing his big red nose and his make-up. He turned and looked at Mama and said, "I never touched that thing."

The owner of the station, Peter Abasi, had been watching the show. He approached the group, then looked at Mukanda and said, "Then where in the world *is* it?"

Ruta Garama had been accompanied by a woman from the National Museum, where the sculpture is kept. She was a tall lady who walked using a pair of crutches that clipped onto her arms.

"We need to seal the building," the woman from the National Museum said. "Now! And then someone needs to call the police."

The station owner, Mr. Abasi, looked around and snapped his fingers. "Do it!" he shouted.

A few minutes later a very, very tall and very, very thin man with very black skin swept into the room. He had a pipe clenched in his teeth and his chin tilted up into the air. I recognized him as Inspector Ignatius Sang, the most famous police detective in Kenya. He had even been on our show once. He told us all about what it was like to be a policeman. Inspector Sang was followed by six uniformed Kenya police officers.

"Seal the building!" he said again. His voice was not loud, and yet when he spoke, everyone listened. "Don't let anyone leave."

tatu

*S*o Lulu," Baba said, smiling at me over breakfast the next morning, "I hear Ignatius Sang gave you the third degree." I call my father Baba.

"He was a little scary," I agreed as our maid, Kanze, set my bowl of Wheatabix cereal on the table in front of me. Thinking back, the detective hadn't frowned or looked mean . . . but there was something about him that made me very nervous.

"A very impressive man," Mama added. "Very thorough."

My father lifted up his copy of the *Daily Nation*. On the cover was the headline: "Famous Sculpture Stolen on Live TV!" Under that, in smaller letters, it said, "World's Funniest Clown Not Laughing Anymore."

I frowned, stared at the headline, then read

the first few paragraphs. Suddenly I felt a little sick. "What?" I yelled. "No. That can't be!"

"What do you mean?" Baba said.

"They're saying Mukanda did it. He'd never do anything like that!"

Baba read the article carefully. "They're not saying he's been arrested," he said. "Just that he's a suspect."

My little brother, Charles, added, "If Ignatius Sang thinks Mukanda did it, then he did it. Ignatius Sang always gets his man!"

"How would you know?" I asked angrily. Charles wasn't on *KenyaKidz* and rarely came to the broadcasts, so he didn't really know Mukanda. "Mukanda wouldn't steal a shilling if you dropped it right in front of his face."

"I bet he would!" Charles said. "Plus, he's not even a very funny clown."

"Yes, he is!"

"No, he's not!"

"Yes, he is!"

"No, he's not!"

"Enough," my father said.

"Mukanda's the nicest. . . ."

"Enough!" My father slapped the paper down on the table, then stood up. "Elias," he called to our driver, who was eating breakfast in the next room, "pull the car around, would you? I'll be ready to go in a few minutes."

We have four servants: Elias the driver, Ruth the cook, Monte the gardener, and Kanze, our maid.

"Mukanda's a Kalenjin," Charles said. "Everybody knows they're all a bunch of thieves."

In Kenya we have about forty different tribes and ethnic groups. My family is from the Kikuyu tribe, which is the biggest. Everybody says that Kikuyus are good at making money and that Luos are smart but showy. And that Kalenjins are thieves. It's silly to say that all people in one group would all act the same.

"That's not true!" I said. "My friend Amina is a Kalenjin. She never steals anything."

"You're just defending her because she's your best friend," Charles said. "All I know is *I* don't leave money lying around when she comes over."

"You're such a pig!" I said.

"Charles, those are just old stories," Mama said.

"Still, I bet Mukanda stole that moldy old sculpture. He's a Kalenjin."

"You want to bet?" I put out my hand. "Five shillings says Mukanda didn't do it."

"*Ten* shillings," Charles said.

We shook hands.

Charles jumped up and turned on the TV. The news was just coming on.

The newscaster, a distinguished-looking man with a touch of gray hair at his temples, was saying, "Inspector Ignatius Sang may have already cracked the case. While police are still searching for the missing artwork by noted sculptor Ruta Garama, an arrest appears to be pending. National police this morning briefly detained Mukanda Ngilu. While the suspect has not yet been formally charged, Mr. Ngilu, beloved by children across Kenya for his portrayal of Mukanda, the World's Funniest Clown —"

Charles switched off the TV and held out his palm toward me. "I want my ten shillings, Lulu."

No, I thought. *It's not possible. Not Mukanda.*

"Ten shillings," Charles said, slapping his palm loudly. Charles is probably the most irritating little brother in the whole world.

"He didn't do it," I said.

"Pay up. I want my ten shillings."

"He didn't do it," I said. Ten shillings isn't much. It's only about a little more than a dime in American money. But still, I just didn't believe it.

"Mukanda didn't do it. And I'm going to prove it!"

"Oh, really?" Charles's voice was sarcastic. "And precisely how do you intend to do that?"

"Uh . . . ." I said. Well, that was brilliant.

That day after school, I went to the studio with Mama to tape a segment for her TV show. As I passed the small room where Mukanda put on his make-up, I looked in and saw him sitting miserably in his chair. His dreadlocks hung over his face and he was looking down at the floor.

I knocked gently and walked in. Mukanda looked up, swept back his dreadlocks, and smiled. But it was a sad smile. He didn't have his make-up on. Without it, Mukanda always looks serious. But today he looked more serious than usual.

"Lulu!" he said. His tone was cheerful, but I could tell he wasn't really happy.

I went over and took his hand. "I know you didn't do it," I said.

He nodded. "Unfortunately I can't prove it."

"How could you have taken it?" I said. "The lights weren't off for more than ten seconds."

He shrugged. "They seem to think I took it and put it in the back room." He pointed. "Over there. The one next to the back door. They say an accomplice came and took it while we were still doing the show."

"But it was totally dark in there!" I said. "There was no way you could see."

"Yes!" Mukanda nodded sharply. "That's what I keep telling Inspector Sang. I keep saying, 'Explain to me, Detective Sang, exactly how I could see in the dark.' It makes no sense! How could I steal it if I couldn't see?" Mukanda whacked his palms angrily on the arms of his chair.

"Indeed," a voice behind us said, "that is the question."

A shadow fell across the room. I turned and saw a man standing in the door.

It was Inspector Sang. He was so tall his head nearly touched the top of the door. He was holding a straight-stemmed pipe, unlit, in one hand.

Mukanda and I stared at him.

"According to everyone's testimony, it was pitch dark. Impossible to see." The detective raised both eyebrows. "And yet someone must have been able to see. Otherwise, they could not have stolen a fifty-pound sculpture and carried it across the room without tripping or dropping it."

"But how is that possible?" I asked.

Inspector Sang put the pipe between his

teeth, reached into his green coat, and pulled out a piece of paper with several stamps on it. "This warrant," he said, "authorizes me to search this room."

"I have nothing to hide!" Mukanda declared.

Inspector Sang stepped aside and nodded at someone. Two large, uniformed constables walked into the room. The first one went straight to the desk where Mukanda stored his clown suit, pulled out the suit, and flung it on the floor. Underneath it was a strange looking mask of some sort. There was a rubber part that went over the face, two round glass pieces where the eyes should be, and a bunch of elastic straps.

The officer smiled. "Here they are." He picked them up and handed them to Inspector Sang.

"Night vision goggles," the detective said, holding the mask out at arm's length. "They're used by the military to see in the dark." He lifted them up and ran his finger across the rubber rim of the goggles. The tip of his finger came away stained bright red. "Grease paint." The detective gave Mukanda a significant look. "Just like a clown wears."

Mukanda stood up as though he was getting ready to run out of the room. One of the uniformed police officers stepped in his path.

"Mukanda Ngilu," Inspector Sang said, "you are under arrest for theft, as well as violations of the National Treasures Act. Please turn around."

Mukanda didn't move. The two officers took him by the shoulders, turned him around, and twisted his arms behind his back. He grimaced as they handcuffed him. "This isn't right!" he said. "It wasn't me!"

Inspector Sang set the night vision goggles on the desk, then pulled out a handkerchief and wiped his red-stained finger on it. "Place these into evidence, constable," he said to one of the officers.

Then he turned and swept out of the room.

Seeing that a terrible injustice has been done, Lulu flings herself against the brutal policemen who are dragging away the innocent man.

With a flurry of judo throws, she subdues the misguided policemen. Mukanda stands in the middle of the hallway, staring at her in shock. "I didn't know you could fight like that!" he says.

"Run, Mukanda!" she yells. As Lulu holds the police at bay with her brilliant martial arts skills, Mukanda sprints for the back door.

"I'll never forget you, Lulu!" he shouts, before disappearing out the back door.

I sighed and drifted slowly back to reality. The room was empty, Mukanda's wrinkled clown suit still lying in a pathetic heap on the floor. He was really going to jail. How was this possible? It wasn't right!

I had to do *something*. But what?

nne

When we got home from the studio, Mama said, "Don't forget, we're all going over to Peter Abasi's house for dinner tonight."

Charles groaned. I groaned. My father groaned.

"My feet itch every time I look at that man!" Baba said. Any time my father doesn't like something, he says it makes his feet itch.

"Look, he's the director of KenyaTV," Mama said. "I can't very well say no when he invites us over to dinner."

My father rolled his eyes and sighed. But Mama was right. Not only was Mr. Abasi the best known news anchorman in Kenya, but he was the owner of the station. He could get rid of the *KenyaKidz* show with a snap of his fingers.

It was never any fun going over to visit, though. His children were the same age as Charles and me. And they pretty much spent the entire time we were with them telling us how great they were, how much money they had, or showing us their new toys. (But not letting us play with them!)

Two hours later we were in the living room of Mr. Abasi's house. The family lived in a huge house the color of mint toothpaste in the ritzy suburb of Muthaiga. The green house was surrounded by a ten-foot-high wall and a very large, carefully landscaped piece of property. As usual, Mr. Abasi started the conversation by bragging about his son, Amos, who is my age.

"He's a champion footballer!" Mr. Abasi said, his arm around Amos's shoulder. Amos gave us all a smug smile. Like his father, Amos is very handsome. And like his father, he's totally full of himself.

"Show them the trophy," Mrs. Abasi said. "Daniel!" Mr. Abasi snapped his fingers impatiently at one of their servants. "Daniel! Bring the trophy!"

Daniel was one of about ten servants the Abasis had working at their house. The Abasis were always yelling at them. Once, I even saw Amos throw one of his toys at a servant. But his parents didn't get angry. In fact, they didn't seem to think of their servants as people.

The butler, Daniel, scurried off, then hustled back with a trophy in his hands.

"Isn't that nice," my mother said. "Lulu loves football, too."

"Really!" Mr. Abasi said. "A girl footballer, eh?" He gave me a condescending look. This was only about the tenth time Mama had told him I was crazy for football. He never remembered. "Maybe the children could have a quick game in the backyard. Go get your ball, Amos."

A few minutes later, we were playing a game in Mr. Abasi's backyard. It was me and Charles against Amos and his little brother, Anthony. The Abasis had a huge piece of property, with the servants' house in one corner, some big bougainvillea trees blazing with red flowers here and there, and the rest composed of perfectly flat, perfectly manicured grass. It was better than most football fields.

Several of the servants ran out and immediately started setting up a field for us to play on. They actually had a machine for making lines and two miniature practice goal nets that appeared from a shed near the servants' house. Within

minutes there was a miniature field, perfect for playing two-on-two.

"Go easy on her, Amos," Mr. Abasi called as we started to play. "She's just a girl!"

Well! I had figured I would lose to Amos to begin with. But after Mr. Abasi said that, I was determined that Charles and I were going to stomp Amos and his brother into the ground. The problem was, Charles hates football. He just likes to read and study. He's kind of a brainiac, actually.

"First team to score three goals wins!" Mr. Abasi called, booting the ball onto the field.

We started playing. Amos tried to dodge around me a couple of times and seemed to be surprised when, each time, he was unsuccessful. Once he realized that I was better than he'd expected, I could see him trying to figure out another way to beat me.

He came up with a strategy pretty quickly. He ran straight toward Charles, screening me. There was no way to keep defending him without smashing into Charles. I had to pull up short as Amos raced toward the goal. He dribbled the ball all the way into the goal.

"Scoooooooore!" he yelled, doing an annoying victory dance in front of the goal.

I grabbed Charles. "Don't let him do that again!" I hissed. "If he tries that again, step in his way."

After that, Amos spent a few minutes showing off what a great dribbler he was, shaking his butt and making goofy faces while he tried to get past me. I was determined it wouldn't happen, though.

After I'd stolen the ball from him for about the third time, I could see he was starting to get frustrated. So he did the same thing that he'd done before, using Charles as a screen. Again, Charles just stood there cluelessly, blocking me out so that I couldn't cover Amos as he darted toward the goal.

Two to nothing.

More butt shaking and arm waving and taunting laughter from Amos.

"Charles!" I whispered. "Don't let him do that."

"It's just a game," Charles said. "Who cares if he wins?"

I care! I thought. But I didn't say anything.

I took the ball downfield, shook off Anthony, then took a long shot at the corner of the goal. Amos was so busy trying to look cool he didn't get to the ball. It bounced off his foot and went in.

"I could have gotten that," he said, pouting. "I just *let* you have it."

"Right," I said, sarcasm dripping everywhere.

For a while, Anthony and Charles might as well not have been on the field. It was just me and Amos. He was bigger and faster than me. But he had two weaknesses in his game. First, he didn't keep his cool. And second, he thought he was better than he was. I've learned those are both things that you can use against a player. If a person like that gets frustrated, he gets mad. Then he starts making mistakes.

Amos started trying to beat me on pure speed. So I just played him loose, staying between him and the goal.

"You're cheating," he said. "You're not even trying to score. You're just playing defense."

"Really?" I said, stealing the ball from him as he made a big cut and tried to blaze past me. I passed to Charles. Charles headed for the sideline, pulling Anthony away from the goal. Then Charles—miraculously!—sent me a perfect pass. I took the shot and scored.

"Two to two," I said, smiling. "Who's playing defense now?"

I could see Amos was boiling mad. He hated to lose. But then, I can't blame him—so do I.

Amos got the ball again, dribbled around a

little, not even pretending to try passing to his brother. I could see what he was going to do from a mile away. He was going to screen out with Charles again.

But this time I was ready. I dropped back as Amos cut toward the center of the field, heading toward Charles. Amos's face was determined, his eyes narrowed. He had that nothing-is-getting-in-my-way look in his eyes.

But this time, instead of standing there like a lump, Charles took one step forward, directly into Amos's path.

Oh no! I thought. *I never should have said anything.*

Amos didn't even slow down. He just smashed into Charles. Charles is only eight, while Amos is a very large eleven-year-old. Charles didn't have a chance. He flew through the air and landed on the ground flat on his back.

I suppose I should have gone straight to Charles to make sure he was okay. But I knew that Amos had done it on purpose. Amos turned toward the goal without even pausing to look at Charles. His arms were swinging back and forth, and his head was lowered. His legs pumped as he sped toward the goal.

Even though I had repositioned myself,
expecting this, I could see he was too fast for me.

There was only one thing to do.

Slide tackle.

I slid toward him, one foot sticking out in
front of me. My shoe contacted the ball . . . which
stopped moving, slamming the ball into Amos's
feet. Amos's feet stopped suddenly. The rest of him,
however, kept going.

Next thing I knew, Amos was airborne, flying
over my head and then crashing to the ground
with a thud. I jumped to my feet and kicked the
ball all the way down the field. It rolled toward

the goal, slowing, slowing, slowing. It stopped just inches past the line.

I saw Daniel, the servant, near the goal. He pointed toward the goal line—the signal for a goal.

"Three to two," I said matter of factly. "We win."

As I turned away from the goal, I heard a terrible wail. I assumed it was Charles. But Charles was standing up, dusting himself off like nothing had happened.

Amos, on the other hand, was holding his shin and writhing around on the ground. "Foul!" he screamed. "She tripped me! She's a cheater!"

All our parents and all the servants ran over and stood around him.

"Cheater! Cheater!" Amos continued to scream. Tears were running down his face now.

"What were you thinking, little girl?" Mr. Abasi asked, looking at me coldly.

"It was a legal tackle," I said. "I never touched anything but the ball."

"Legal or not," Mama chimed in, "you can't go tripping people!"

I looked at my father for help. Mama didn't know anything about football. But Baba knew it was a fair tackle. He just shrugged.

"Baba!"

"Let it go," Baba said.

Amos's mother scooped Amos up in her arms, gave me a dirty look, then carried her son across the yard as he sobbed. I thought he was playing it up a little too much. Sure, he'd taken a fall. But I was pretty sure he wasn't really hurt.

I heard Mrs. Abasi mutter something to him about "that mean, nasty little girl" as she carried him across the grass.

"Lulu, go and sit in the car," Mama said.

"Mama," I said, "I didn't do anything wrong! Baba tell her."

"Just go sit in the car," Baba said.

Of course, it turned out that Amos was fine. The only thing he'd hurt was his pride. When I was finally released from the car, I found Amos back inside playing the latest video game from Japan on his father's huge new wide-screen television.

He and Anthony were playing a game where these two guys with giant muscles karate chop and punch and kick each other until finally one of their heads flies off and blood spurts all over the place.

"Have they let you play yet?" I asked Charles.

He shook his head. We watched the two brothers play for a minute.

Hah! Uh! Whack! Whack! Whack! Yah! Uh! Hah! Whack! The video game kept making the same sounds over and over as the two fighters on the screen thumped on each other. I couldn't see why anybody would want to play a game like that. It was about the dumbest thing I'd ever seen.

"What do you want to do?" I asked Charles. He shrugged, then went over to the bookshelf, found a book about elephants, and started reading. I stood there for a minute while Amos and Anthony karate chopped each other. *Hah! Uh! Uh! Whack! Uh! Whack! Hah! Yee! Uh! Hah!*

Finally I got so bored that I went into the living room where all the grown-ups were. I sat down on the floor.

As usual, Mr. Abasi was talking. "I've just gotten a new piece," he said. "This one's by a Nigerian artist." Mr. Abasi had a big collection of African art and he was always telling you about his latest acquisition. And how much it cost. Everything Mr. Abasi had, he had to tell you how much it cost.

He showed off a big painting of a woman in traditional dress grinding corn. You could see all the muscles in her arms, and her eyes were all lit up like she was doing something really fun and amazing. Mama is big on having me learn about traditional ways of doing things, like cooking. So I've ground corn plenty of times. And, trust me, grinding corn is not fun at all.

"Nine hundred thousand shillings!" Mr. Abasi said. "But worth every shilling, don't you think?"

"My goodness," Mama said. "Isn't that nice." I could tell by the way she said it that she didn't really think so.

We sat silently for a minute, looking at his nine hundred thousand shillings' worth of art. Then he said, "All right then, I'll put it away."

He took out his keys, picked up the painting, and carried it out of the room. When he returned, he  said, "I keep all my art locked up." He held up the key. "This is the only key, too. I won't even let my servants into that room."

Baba looked at me and rolled his eyes. I could tell Baba wanted to get home as much as I did.

"The events at the studio yesterday remind us

how careful one must be," Mr. Abasi said. "Why, only last year I was offered a work of art by a legitimate art dealer. I found out later that it had been stolen from a private collector in South Africa."

"What's the point of having art if you keep it all locked up in a room?" Baba asked.

"Fair question," Mr. Abasi said, laughing but not really looking like he thought it was funny. "But if I left it unprotected, the Mukandas of the world would be in here robbing me blind."

"I suppose so," Baba said.

"Speaking of Mukanda, Betty," Mr. Abasi said to Mama. "We'll need to officially fire him. I'll have a statement prepared to broadcast tomorrow."

I couldn't help thinking how unfair this was. And Mama didn't say *anything!*

Mr. Abasi shook his head. "Tragic, tragic. Such a talented young man. You know he's a musician, don't you?"

Mrs. Abasi cut in. "Musician or not, he's trash. Good riddance to bad rubbish!"

"I never saw any evidence that he was dishonest," Mama said.

"Besides, he's a Kalenjin," Mrs. Abasi said. "My mother always used to say that even if you sacrificed a goat with a Kalenjin and became their most trusted friend — some day they'll come back and steal something from you. Just because they can." She clapped her hands loudly.

"Daniel? Mr. and Mrs. Kibwana's glasses are empty! More drinks for our guests."

"Look," Mr. Abasi said to Mama, "I've known a few decent Kalenjin. But most of them. . ." He spread his hands helplessly.

Mrs. Abasi waved one hand dismissively. "Trash. They're trash."

"They're not trash!" I said. "Mukanda is nice. I don't think he stole *anything*."

Suddenly the room was quiet. All the adults turned and looked at me. The silence seemed to stretch on and on.

"When I was a girl," Mrs. Abasi said finally, "children were to be seen and not heard."

"I'm sorry," Mama said. "She's a very strong-minded girl."

"Well, I don't think it's right!" I said. "Until he's been proven guilty in court, he should be presumed innocent."

Mr. Abasi looked at me with a thin smile on his face. "Well, well! Not only a footballer, but a budding lawyer as well. Is there anything she can't do?"

"I'm going to find out who did it, Mr. Abasi," I said. "Because I don't think it was Mukanda."

Mr. Abasi's smile faded. "There are some matters that are best left in the hands of grown-ups." It sounded like a warning.

I felt my lips pressing together.

"Lulu," Mama said, "it's time for you to go play with the others."

I could hear the video game from the other room. *Uh! Whack! Hah! Whack! Whack! Aaaaghhh!*

"Yes, ma'am," I said.

Mama seemed annoyed as we drove home. "Why do you have to antagonize him?" she said to Baba.

"Antagonize? I just made a few jokes."

"You pointed out what a fool he is," Mama said.

"It's not exactly hard to do," Baba said.

"Yes, but it's not your show that will get cancelled if he decides he doesn't like me anymore. This thing with Mukanda just gives him all the more reason not to trust my judgment."

Baba didn't say anything.

"And Lulu's little performance beating up

Amos didn't help," she added as we drove down our street and approached the house.

"Beating him up!" I said. "I tackled him. Totally legally. All I touched was the ball."

Mama pursed her lips but didn't say anything.

When we reached our house, we honked the horn and Elias came out to open the gate and let us in. Charles had fallen asleep in the back seat. We parked and Mama carried Charles into the house.

"I thought it was a superb tackle myself," Baba whispered to me.

We both giggled as we walked into the house.

CHAPTER FIVE

tano

The next day I had a stroke of good luck. It turned out that my entire class at school was going to the National Museum. That would give me a chance to do some investigating!

The museum was pretty interesting. There were masks and statues from many different tribal groups. As I mentioned before, there are 40 different tribes and ethnic groups in Kenya. Some are big, but some have only a few hundred people in them. The national language is Kiswahili, but in my school most of the teaching is done in English. Most people also speak their own tribal languages, too.

Anyway, the museum had arts and crafts made by most of the different ethnic groups in the country, and that's what we went to see. "Are we going to see any of the modern art?" I asked Miss Nyende, my teacher.

"I don't think we'll have time," she said.

That's when I decided to sneak off by myself. I looked at the museum map and saw that there was a special exhibition of art by Ruta Garama. I waited until Miss Nyende was looking the other way, then I quickly snuck off. My heart was pounding in my chest, but I couldn't help myself.

I followed the map until I reached the Special Exhibition Hall, a room with a high ceiling on the first floor of the museum. I peeked in nervously. There were some paintings on the wall and several sculptures. These sculptures were much bigger than the one that had been stolen from the TV studio. But they were similar in that they were all fierce looking figures—forbidding-looking bronze people, their eyes staring angrily at me.

As soon as I saw them, I started wondering why I had come there. What had I hoped to find out? The larger version of the stolen sculpture wasn't even *here*. A nervous feeling ran through me. I decided I had to go right back up to join my class. I was sure to get into trouble if I didn't get back soon.

Just as I was about to leave, I heard a strange thumping noise. I turned around to see a pleasant-faced woman with lots of jingly bracelets around

41

both wrists rounding the corner. She leaned heavily on a pair of crutches. It was the lady from the museum who had accompanied Mr. Garama to the television studio. She looked at me curiously. "Are you lost?" she said.

"Sort of," I said.

She looked at me for a moment. "Do I know you?" she asked.

"I'm Lulu Kibwana. I was at the KenyaTV studio when the sculpture was stolen."

Her face grew serious. "Ah, of course. You're Miss Betty's daughter. You had a football in your hand the whole time you were there."

I smiled. "That's right!"

"My name is Joyce Mehada. I'm assistant director of the museum. We're quite distressed about the loss of the sculpture."

"Well . . . actually that's why I'm here," I said. "I'm investigating."

Her eyebrows went up. "Investigating?"

"Yes, I'm trying to find out what happened to the sculpture."

Mrs. Mehada gave me the sort of smile that grown-ups give you when they think you're doing something really cute and silly. "Well, my goodness," she said. "But you know, they've already arrested the young man who did it. It was that clown on your show."

I was about to say that I was sure that Mukanda hadn't done it. But it struck me that if I wanted to know who *really* did it, it might be better not to admit that. That way people would think I was just some little kid who didn't know anything.

"But you still haven't found the sculpture, have you?"

"It is puzzling," she said. "Obviously this clown, Mukanda, didn't do it alone. Someone was helping him."

"Why do you say that?" I said.

"There wasn't time for him to take it all the way out of the building. The lights were only off for about ten seconds." She narrowed her eyes thoughtfully. "No, he might be working with a whole gang of thieves."

"A *gang*?"

"Oh, yes. Stealing art isn't easy. It usually takes several people to steal a piece of art."

"What do you think they did with it?"

"Oh, they'll sell it to a collector."

"So if you could find out who would want to buy a sculpture like that. . ."

Mrs. Mehada pointed her finger at me, her bracelets jangling against her crutch. "Smart girl! That's right. If we found who might want to buy the sculpture, we'd know."

"Can you think of anyone?"

"Well, there are thousands of people who collect modern African art, and they're scattered all across the world. America, Japan, Europe, Nigeria, South Africa. . ."

"So you think it's going to be smuggled into another country?"

"Who knows? We do have major collectors here, too, of course. And the subject matter—the fact that it was the model for the sculpture that's in front of the parliament building—well, that might suggest a Kenyan collector."

"Like who?"

"Most of them are high government officials. Some businessmen." She smiled. "Peter Abasi, of course, from the TV station, is a major collector." She frowned. "In fact, now that I think of it, he actually contacted the museum once to find out if he could purchase the sculpture."

That was interesting! I thought about the fact that he had all of his art hidden away in a locked room. If he felt like having something stolen for him, he could put it in that room and no one would ever know he had it.

"Well, maybe *he* was the one who stole it!" I blurted out.

She smiled. "Mr. Abasi is a very respectable man. It hardly seems likely he would be involved in a thing like this."

"I guess," I said.

She frowned. "Still . . . he was *quite* interested in the piece. In fact, he pulled a few strings with people on the board of directors of the museum in an attempt to get the museum to release the piece for purchase." She waved her hand at the room full of art. "Nothing ever came of it, though."

"Why not?"

"It was the model for the most famous sculpture in this country. It's probably the most valuable sculpture ever made by a Kenyan. So naturally the museum wants to hold onto it."

"I see."

"I mean, the reality is, everybody wants it. Not just Mr. Abasi."

"Like who?"

"Well, Ruta Garama, for one."

That was strange. "But he *made* it! If he wants it, why did he sell it in the first place?"

"It's a long story. But the bottom line is that he claims that the museum didn't pay him properly for it. So he wants it back. As a matter of fact, he already stole it once."

"What?" I said. "Do the police know this?"

"Long story," she said.

"Another suspect!" I said. "He was in the studio when it disappeared, too."

"I've known Ruta Garama for years. In fact, he was my sculpture teacher when I was studying art in college. He has a temper. Sometimes he can be a little unreasonable. But of course, he's an artist. And he's honest. He wouldn't have stolen it."

"But you said he stole it before."

"Like I said, it's a long story. I'm quite convinced he wouldn't do it again."

"But that's true of Mukanda, too," I protested. "He's such a nice person."

"Well, I don't know him," Mrs. Mehada said. "So I can't say."

"Okay, so let's rule out Mr. Garama. Still, Mr. Abasi could just as easily have done it as Mukanda."

"Yes, but look at the two of them. You may like this clown, but his background sounds a bit sketchy. According to the newspapers, he used to be in a gang in Mathare. He was a street boy, they say."

I had never heard anything like that. Mukanda? Pleasant, friendly, polite Mukanda— a *street boy*? It didn't seem to add up. "Everybody makes mistakes," I said. "I know he's from a very poor background. But that doesn't mean he's a criminal."

Mrs. Mehada looked thoughtful. "I wonder. . . ." she said.

"What?"

"Our priority at the museum is simply to get the sculpture back. I wonder. . . ." Then she shook her head. "No. No, that's quite impossible."

"What is?"

She had an odd expression on her face as she

looked at me. "Well, if you really are friends with this Mukanda. . ."

"Yes?"

"I talked to Inspector Sang today, and he said that in many cases he's able to crack a suspect by having them talk to a family member or a friend. Sometimes a friend can talk sense into a person more easily than a policeman can."

"I don't understand."

"I think the police would be prepared to be lenient with Mukanda if he would give up the names of the people he was working with." She frowned. "So it occurred to me that perhaps *you* could talk to him and. . . ." Then she shook her head a second time. "No. Never mind. You're only a little girl. It's completely unreasonable of me to put a child in the position of going into a prison and. . . ." She looked around. "Where *are* the rest of the children in your group?"

Suddenly I had an idea. She was right. Maybe Inspector Sang would let me talk to Mukanda! If Mukanda *did* steal the sculpture—which I was sure he didn't—I might be able to help him get a lighter punishment. But if not, he might have seen something or heard something that would help my investigation.

"I'd better go!" I said.

"Nice meeting you, Lulu!" she called, her bracelets jingling as she waved good-bye to me.

I ran through the museum until I saw two lines of girls on the far side of one of the exhibit halls, all of them wearing blue skirts and blue jackets like mine. They were just lining up to head back to the bus.

I just made it! Boy, would I have been in trouble if I'd missed the bus. I jumped into line, my heart pounding.

"Oh, there you are, Lulu!" Miss Nyende said, smiling at me. "Where were you?"

"Who me?" I asked.

sita

*T*hump. *Thump. Thump. Thump.*

Mama and I were pounding corn in the *kinu*. In Africa, women grind corn for cornbread and other kinds of food in a *kinu*. A *kinu* is basically a large piece of stone with a bowl at the top. You fill it with dried corn. Then you lift a heavy stick up in the air and bring it down—*thump*—on top of the corn. Eventually it grinds up all the corn.

You can buy ground corn at the store, but Mama swears it tastes better this way. I always complain about grinding corn. But there is something kind of nice about doing it with Mama. We stand facing each other and we have to get into a rhythm or we'll bang into each other. Despite all my complaining, there is something comforting about it.

"You look sad," Mama said after we'd been pounding away for a while.

"I keep thinking about poor Mukanda. I just don't think he did it," I said.

"You keep saying that," she said. "But why else would those night vision goggles have been in his drawer?"

That was a question I'd thought about a lot. And I'd come up with an answer. "Maybe somebody put them there. Somebody who wanted to make it look like he was the one."

"Doesn't that seem a little unlikely?"

"Think of it from his point of view, though," I said. "If he really stole the sculpture, he wouldn't have kept the goggles in his desk. He had to know there was a good chance the police would search his office. He would have gotten them out of the TV station as soon as possible."

"He had to put them somewhere. I bet those goggles cost forty or fifty thousand shillings. He wouldn't have just thrown them in the rubbish bin. Besides, the police have found out a lot about him that we didn't know before. He was arrested several times when he was younger."

"That was a long time ago."

"And he was in a gang."

Thump. Thump. Thump. Thump.

"I think we should go talk to him," I said.

Mama blinked. "*Talk* to him! Why on earth would we do that?"

"You know he doesn't have any family," I said. "Don't you think somebody should be helping him. We could take him some food and lift his spirits a little. What could be wrong with that?"

Mama looked thoughtful. "Well, that's a very decent thing for you to suggest. I might consider going myself. But bringing a little girl to jail? I wouldn't even consider it."

Thump. Thump. Thump.

Suddenly I felt tears coming out of my eyes, running down my face.

"Look what you're doing!" Mama said. "You're dripping into the *kinu*!"

I dropped the pounding stick and hid my face in my hands. I couldn't even say quite why I felt so sad. But I wanted to help Mukanda so much.

Mama set her stick down and put her arms around me. "All right," she said finally. "We have to shoot that story about the Mathare football team tomorrow. I'll take you to the jail to see Mukanda tomorrow on the way."

I felt a burst of happiness. "Yay! Yay! Yay!" I jumped up and down.

* * *

You might wonder why I cared so much about helping Mukanda. Here's why.

The reason I came on the show was that an older girl quit so she could concentrate on her school work. I was her replacement. When I first came on the show, the other kids had been on the show for a long time. They all seemed to be friends. And I was always the odd one out. It seemed like they were always making jokes about me, about what I wore, about how I was always off in Lulu Land, about how I forgot my lines. The only person who was really nice to me was Mukanda.

Some kids might have quit the show. But I just tried harder and harder to fit in. I tried to wear clothes like Grace Awino. I tried to talk like Martha Kariuki. I tried to make jokes like Mukanda.

Then I would look at the tapes and I could see I was awful. I stuck out like a sore thumb. I was a total failure. Everybody else on the show seemed so natural, but I just seemed ridiculous.

Most of the kids on the show got mail from kids around the country. They would always tell Grace how beautiful she was or Martha how smart she was. I never seemed to get any mail at all.

Then one day I was helping my mother and I

found a stack of mail in an envelope with Diana, the name of the girl I'd replaced, written on it. I opened it up and looked at the notes. They said things like, "Why is Lulu on the show? We hate her. We want Diana back." There were some that were even worse. It was obvious Mama had hidden them from me. I felt so embarrassed! Everybody in Kenya hated me.

I started crying. Mukanda was walking by the office and he saw me huddled in the chair, bawling away. He came in, sat down, and in his soft voice said, "What's wrong?"

I handed him the letters. He read every single one of them without speaking. Finally he put them back in the envelope and dropped them in the trash. "You know what the problem is?"

I shook my head.

"You're trying to be someone you're not."

I didn't understand what he meant.

He smiled, his warm brown eyes looking straight into mine. "Let Grace be the glamorous one. Let Martha be the clever one who always knows the answers. Let me be the prankster. You need to be you."

"But what's that *mean*?" I cried.

"Every time I see you outside the studio,

you're playing with this." He held up the football. I
looked at the white ball, its black spots worn gray
from all the times I'd kicked it. He handed it to me.
"You, Lulu, you're the girl with the football."

"But everybody thinks football's for boys. If I
went on the show with a football, they'd just laugh
at me!"

"What do you dream about?" he asked.

"Football," I said.

"Then just try it," he said. "I have faith in you.
When I look at you, I see a beautiful girl who loves
something a lot. I think when the rest of Kenya

sees what I see . . ." He smiled, then gave me a big hug. "They're going to love you."

And he was right. From that show on, I always wore a football jersey and carried a football on the set. And within a month or two, I started getting mail from all over Kenya. Little girls would write to me saying how much they loved football. How they wanted to play but the boys wouldn't let them. How they had started a team in their village. How they had started playing at their school. They told me I inspired them! Can you believe that? Me? I actually inspired people. Just by being myself!

I started doing better in school. I started smiling more. I even got better at football.

And I had Mukanda to thank for it.

After what he'd done for me, I just couldn't let him down.

saba

The next day, Mama picked me up from school. Her cameraman from *KenyaKidz*, Arthur, was driving a Land Rover with the KenyaTV logo on the side.

"We're just going to make a *very* quick stop at the jail," she said. "Then we'll go to Mathare and shoot the football video for the show."

I had never seen the central jail in Nairobi before. It was a ramshackle place with high walls topped with rusting barbed wire. "This place was built by the British back when Kenya was still a British colony," the cameraman said. That was almost fifty years ago. "I don't believe it's received a lick of paint since then."

There was a crowd of poorly dressed women milling around at the entrance. Many of them carried ragged white bags in their hands. "They're waiting for visiting hour," Arthur said. He was also a cameraman for KenyaTV's news programs. "They're only allowed in one hour a day. But the prison changes the hour every day. Prisoners' families bring them food. There's food inside the prison, but it's not very good. So sometimes these women have to wait all day."

"Do we have to wait, too?" I asked.

"No, no," the cameraman said. "Only the poor people have to wait. We'll pay a small service fee to the warden, and we'll be allowed right in."

We drove through a gate guarded by policemen carrying rifles. Some of the poor women tried to rush in behind us. But the policemen pushed them back with their rifles. The gates closed slowly behind us.

As we opened our car doors, a powerful smell hit me. It smelled like unwashed bodies and garbage. "Pee-yew!"

"You can stay in the car if you want," Mama said.

I shook my head.

One of the policemen escorted us into a building that said ADMINISTRATION on the side. A jolly looking man in a very nice suit was waiting for us inside the door.

"Mrs. Kibwana!" he said. "What a great

pleasure, ma'am! I'm Warden Muge. My daughter is a great, great fan of your show." He chatted warmly with Mama as he led us through the building. When we reached the door of a room with the words WARDEN MUGE printed on it in gold letters, he said, "I've taken the liberty of bringing the prisoner to my own office."

"How kind of you," Mama said.

"I'm afraid you'll only be able to spend a few minutes with him."

Mama and I started walking toward the room.

"Oh, goodness!" the warden said. "I'm afraid it's quite out of the question for the young lady to meet with the prisoner."

I looked at my mother. I felt like I was going to cry again. "But. . . ."

Mama put her finger over her lip, then turned to the warden. "She's really very fond of the young man," she said. "I'd take it as a personal favor."

The warden spread his hands. "What can I do? Our policies are quite strict. You do understand? He's quite a notorious criminal. If anything should happen . . . ."

Our cameraman said, "Perhaps an additional guard could be posted for their safety? Maybe an additional fee would be required?"

The warden scratched his head. "Mmmm," he said thoughtfully. "Perhaps something could be arranged." He gestured toward the door. "Go on, ladies. Arthur and I will work out the arrangements."

We went into the room. It was paneled in dark wood and looked like it had come from a building in London. Mukanda sat slumped on a chair, chains around his ankles and wrists. Two very large guards stood behind him, arms behind their backs. He smiled broadly when he saw me. "Lulu! Hello!" Then his smiled faded. "Hello, ma'am." His eyes dropped to the floor.

"Hello, Mukanda," Mama said. "How are you?"

There was a long silence. Mukanda seemed to be struggling to find something to say.

"I am so embarrassed to be here, ma'am," Mukanda said finally. "But you have to believe me. I didn't do this thing!"

"Lulu is quite convinced of it," Mama said, patting me on the shoulder.

"Can I ask you a question, Mukanda?" I said.

Mukanda glanced at Mama, then looked back at me. "Sure, Lulu."

"It seems like they suspected you from the very beginning. Why?"

Mukanda shook his head. "I don't know. I think somebody must have told them something."

"Like who?"

He shook his head. "I don't know."

"Did you ever hear anybody talking about the sculpture before Mr. Garama came?"

"Not really. The curator, Joyce Mehada, came out to the studio to discuss the show. Your mother wasn't there, so she talked to me. She just wanted to make sure that the sculpture could be transported safely into the building."

"Was there anything specific that worried her?"

Mukanda shook his head. "No. She just wanted to see the exact route we would take it through the building. She measured the doors to make sure that the sculpture's crate would fit."

"Did she talk to anyone else?"

Mukanda shook his head, then frowned. "Wait, no, I take it back. Peter Abasi was coming out of his office. He saw Joyce and spoke to her. They seemed to know each other. When she told him that Mr. Garama's sculpture would be on the show, he seemed quite excited."

I was getting more and more suspicious of Mr. Abasi! Which made me think, maybe he was the one who put the blame on Mukanda. "They say in the paper that you were in a gang," I said.

Mukanda shrugged. "I grew up in a bad neighborhood. If you didn't hang out with the other boys in the neighborhood, you got beat up all the time. Was it a gang? Not really. But we did some petty crimes, I'll admit. Stealing from fruit vendors, snatching chains off women on the street. I was arrested twice by the police. I'm ashamed of it now. But it happened, yes."

"Did Mr. Abasi know anything about your past?"

He looked at me curiously. "Why?"

"Just curious," I said.

"Since you ask, yes. He was the one who hired me. You already know that in addition to being the clown on *KenyaKidz*, I'm a recording engineer for the station. When Mr. Abasi hired me, I told him about my past. I thought it was better to be honest than to have it come up later."

"Can you think of anybody who would want to frame you?"

Mukanda shook his head. "No one."

I sighed. This was very disappointing. I guess I was hoping that Mukanda would have the answer that would solve the whole thing. He didn't. If Mr.

Abasi *was* connected to the robbery, I'd have to look elsewhere to find the answers.

"Is there anything we can do for you, Mukanda?" Mama asked.

Mukanda hesitated. "They let me read the newspaper here," he said finally. "It said in the *Nation* this morning that KenyaTV has officially fired me."

Mama nodded. "I'm afraid so."

Mukanda sighed, then stared off into the distance, his face full of sadness. "I am in no position to ask you for anything," he said finally. "But. . ."

"What is it?" Mama said.

"My mother lives in my house with me. She is very ill. Could you possibly look in on her?"

Mama frowned.

"Of course!" I said. "We'd be glad to."

Mama gave me a sharp look. "I'm not sure, Mukanda. Where do you live? Perhaps if it's on the way. . . ."

Mukanda looked embarrassed.

"I'm afraid it's not on the way to anywhere," he said. "I live in Mathare."

Mama looked shocked. "Mathare! What do you mean, you live in Mathare?"

Mathare was where we were shooting our football story. It was also the worst slum in Nairobi. Nobody who worked at KenyaTV lived in a place like Mathare.

"Yes," Mukanda said. "Mathare."

Mama was speechless. Asking someone to go into Mathare was like asking them to go into the jungle. "We're going to Mathare anyway," I said. "We're shooting the football story about the Mathare Youth Sports Association! It'll be perfect."

Mukanda smiled weakly at me, then looked at my mother. "We'll *try*," Mama said. "I can't promise anything."

"My house is near the railroad," he said. "Once you pass the railroad, there's a little grocery store on the corner. Ask at the grocery and they'll be able to tell you how to find it."

Mama cleared her throat. Then there was a long silence. "I don't know what I'm going to do," Mukanda said. "Lulu's right, Miss Betty. Someone must have put those night vision goggles in my office."

"See!" I said.

Mama nodded. But I could see she didn't believe Mukanda. She took a deep breath. "I've spoken with Inspector Sang today," she said. "He tells me that he believes you were working with someone else. He believes that you have been . . . taken advantage of."

Mukanda shook his head sharply. "It's not true!" he said.

"I'm just telling you what Inspector Sang told me," Mama said. "He has told me that he is prepared to be quite lenient with you if you'll tell him who you were working for. There have been several other art thefts recently in Nairobi. He believes there is a gang of art thieves operating in the city. If you help him crack the case —"

Mukanda interrupted by slapping one manacled hand against the arm of his chair. "I can't help him if I didn't do anything!" he shouted. He seemed ready to jump from the chair. One of the burly guards wrapped an arm around his neck.

"Settle down, prisoner!" the guard said.

Mukanda's body slowly relaxed.

"Just tell them *something*," Mama said. "Anything. This is a terrible place. Don't let them throw you in here to rot for the rest of your life!"

Mukanda didn't answer.

The door opened. The warden stood in the doorway. "I'm afraid you'll have to go now, ladies."

"Please!" Mukanda said. "Please look in on my mother!"

As the warden walked us out to our car, I told him that I believed Mukanda was not guilty and that I was going to find out who had really stolen the sculpture.

"My goodness!" the warden said. "We have a budding Ignatius Sang here."

Mama gave the warden a strained smile. "You think she's kidding," Mama said. "The thing about Lulu, she's as stubborn as a zebra."

"In fact I've already found some possible suspects," I said. "For instance, it might interest you to know that Peter Abasi tried to buy the sculpture from the museum several times. And guess how far from the sculpture he was when it disappeared? He was standing in the room next door!"

Mama's mouth kept smiling, but her eyes didn't look happy. "Okay, Lulu, that's enough. Mr. Abasi is *not* a suspect."

"I say he is!" I said.

"What an imagination!" the warden said, laughing. "What an excellent imagination! Aren't children marvelous? The things they say. Mr. Abasi, an art thief? My heavens!" He kept laughing as he opened the door to the car for my mother to get in.

Me, I wanted to punch him in his happy face.

As we drove out of the prison, I said, "I don't understand what happened. Why do the poor people have to wait and we don't?"

"We paid a fee to the warden," Mama said curtly. My mother looked grimly out the window. "Those people can't afford to pay what he asks."

"You mean you *bribed* him?"

Arthur laughed. "It's called a 'special service fee.'"

"Yes, but whatever you call it, the point is, we had to *pay* him just so he'd do his job?"

Mama said nothing.

"There are many ways of doing a job," Arthur said gently from the driver's seat. "Sometimes you have to pay a little extra for people to give you a bit of extra service."

"But that's wrong!" I said. "All those people out there have to stand here all day, just because they're poor. And just because we have a little money we get to walk right in and talk in the warden's private office."

The car was silent for awhile.

"Mathare," Mama said finally. "Why is Mukanda living in Mathare? Mukanda doesn't make a *lot* of money. But he certainly makes enough that he doesn't have to live in a place like Mathare."

"There's only one way to find out," I said.

"How's that?" Mama asked.

"We have to go see his mother."

⚡︎

nane

It turns out that the streets in Mathare have no names. They're not paved. There are no signs, no traffic lights, no neat intersections where one street crosses another. They're just rutted, bare dirt, full of stones and litter. Chickens and dogs root around in trash heaps here and there. So finding a particular house is not easy.

But Arthur seemed to know how to navigate the streets there. He drove fast, blowing his horn all the time, never stopping, never slowing down. He grinned as a group of boys jumped out of the way of the rushing vehicle.

"You almost hit those boys!" I said.

"Stop in this neighborhood," he said laughing, "and those boys will rob us blind."

Mama was looking very nervous.

Suddenly Arthur slammed on the brakes. "There," he said, "I think that's it."

On the corner of the street stood a small cinderblock house. It was painted bright yellow, with a bright red roof. Compared to most of the buildings on the street it looked like a palace— although it was really barely more than a shack.

"Let's make this quick," Arthur said. "This area is not as bad as some. But still. . . ."

We climbed out of the car and knocked on the door. After a moment, a thin woman opened the door and looked out nervously. "Yes?" she said in Kiswahili.

"I'm a friend of Mukanda's," Mama said. "He asked us to come and look in on his mother."

"Oh!" A broad white smile broke out on the young woman's face. "You must be Miss Betty! Come in! Come in!"

She ushered us into to a small, neatly kept room. The furniture was cheap and spare, the sort of thing you can buy from carpenters who make furniture on the streets in Nairobi. On the wall was a picture of Mukanda in his clown costume. The room was divided in half by a flowered curtain that ran down the center.

"Do you mind my asking who you are?" Mama said.

"I'm Millicent, Mukanda's cousin."

Everything about the young woman said that she had recently come here from a village in the country. Her clothes were simple and unflattering, and her Kiswahili was halting and accented.

"I live here and take care of his mother." She pulled back the curtain, revealing a bed. On the bed lay a very old, very sick woman. The old woman's eyes moved, looking at us. She didn't speak.

"Hello Mrs. Ngilu," Mama said.

Mukanda's mother's fingers raised up off the quilt slightly and the corners of her mouth turned up a bit. But other than that, she made no sign that she noticed us.

"You rest, Auntie," Millicent said, pulling the curtain shut.

"And what's wrong with her?" Mama asked softly.

"She's very ill. I don't really understand what the problem is." Millicent scurried around the room, making hot tea for Mama. She served it to her in a cracked teacup on a plate and bowed slightly, the way people out in the villages did when they spoke to a chief or an elder. "She can't walk and can't get out of bed. Mukanda spends all his money on medicine for her, but it doesn't seem to be helping. He has been trying to save enough money for an operation. But he says it will be very, very expensive."

There was a small kitchen area in one corner of the room. But I noticed that the shelves were almost completely bare of food. There was a small bag of rice and a box of biscuits. But that was about all.

The young woman began to cry. "I don't know what we'll do. Mukanda pays for all of this. I read in the paper today that he's to be fired by the station. We'll have no money. His mother will have no one to pay for medicine." She put her face in her hands.

"My father is a doctor," I said. "Maybe he could come and have a look at her."

Mama frowned at me.

"*Could* he?" Millicent asked, brightening slightly.

"That might not be possible," Mama said. "We'll have to talk to him and see what his schedule will allow."

"But. . . . " I began.

"We'll talk to him," Mama said firmly. Then she looked at her watch. "We really have to go now."

The woman fell on her knees and grabbed
Mama's hand. "Please, Miss Betty! You must help
Mukanda! I know he would never do what they
said he did."

"I'll do what I can," Mama said. "He'll have
some pay coming to him. I'll make sure they
get it to him." She opened her purse, took out a
thousand-shilling note, and set it on the table. "In
the meantime. . . ."

"Thank you, Miss Betty!" Mukanda's cousin
said. "Thank you!"

"I'm going to find out who stole that sculpture," I said. "So don't worry."

Millicent looked at me with wide eyes.

"Come on, Lulu," Mama said.

We quickly left the house. Arthur was sitting nervously in the Land Rover. "Well?" he asked.

Mama sighed loudly. "Oh, this is terrible. This is so sad."

"We have to help them!" I said.

Mama made a circle with her hand, indicating the entire area around us. "Lulu," she said, "this whole place is full of people whose lives are even worse than theirs. If you tried to help everybody in Kenya who was suffering, you'd die of exhaustion in a week."

"I'm not talking about everyone," I said. "I just want to help Mukanda and his family."

Mama looked at me sadly, then turned to Arthur. "Let's go. We're already late."

"Am I on?" I asked. As always when I was taping for *KenyaKidz*, I wore my football jersey and carried a black and white spotted ball under my arm. I carried a microphone in my other hand.

"We're rolling," Arthur said. Arthur had set up his camera in front of a small, weedy patch of ground where a bunch of kids were playing football. "The red light is broken."

"Oh," I said. Usually there is a red light that comes on when he is taping. I looked directly into the camera and smiled. "Welcome to Mathare!"

In front of me stretched a wide group of tiny shacks. They were put together from old wooden boards, cardboard boxes, mismatched bricks—anything really. And boy, did it stink! There were no sewers here, no running water. In the distance I could see the tall glass-and-steel towers of Nairobi. But for miles I could see nothing but a clutter of rusting corrugated tin roofs.

"Here in the Mathare section of Nairobi, very few people have much money," I said as the camera continued to tape me. "Most kids can't even afford to buy a football. So a few years ago, the Mathare Youth Sports Association was organized to  help kids here play football. Here's one of their star players, Helen Wako."

The camera panned to a small, thin girl with

short hair and very large eyes who stood in front of me. "Hi!" she said.

"How long have you been playing football, Helen?" I asked.

She laughed. "As long as I can remember."

"With boys?"

"I used to play with boys. But now our association has a girls' division. It's one of the most active girls' football divisions in Kenya."

"I understand you won the most valuable player award this year."

Helen looked a little embarrassed. "Yes," she said.

"You must really be happy."

She nodded. "Yes, but maybe not for the reason you'd think. The association rewards good players with scholarships to school. I couldn't afford to go to a good school without the help of the sports association."

I feel very lucky. My father is a doctor and can afford to send us to good schools. But many kids in Kenya are only able to go to school for a few years, and then they have to drop out. Especially in a place like Mathare.

"All right!" I said. "Let's play some football!" I turned and punted the ball onto the field behind us. A cheer rose from the kids on the field and I ran out and started to play.

Arthur shot video of the game while we played. There was no grass at all—just stones and dirt. I was the only kid on the field who wore cleats. In fact, many of the kids didn't even wear shoes. But they didn't seem to mind. They were really good and it was extremely fun. I play fullback and Helen plays forward, so I was marking her the whole time. She was by far the best girl I'd ever played against. I couldn't believe how quick she was.

At first she beat me to the goal every time. I got a little frustrated. I was a lot bigger than her, so I tried to lean on her. But it was a waste of time. As soon as I got close to her, she just seemed to disappear like smoke. I'd be watching her back as she sprinted toward the goal. But then I started learning how to play her. I had to give her an extra step and force her out toward the wings.

"Lulu!"

At first I didn't even hear my mother, I was concentrating so hard on the game.

"Lulu! Time to go!"

"Maaaama!" I whined. I really wasn't here to play. I was just here to shoot some video. But there isn't anything I'd rather do than play football. So I didn't want to go. "Just a few more minutes!" Helen sped past me and scored another goal.

"Now!" Mama yelled. Her face was angry. I ran toward her.

"Please!" I said. "Just a few more minutes."

"In the car," she said. "*Now.*"

"But —"

"*Now!*" She grabbed my arm and jerked me toward our Land Rover.

That was when I noticed a battered Toyota pickup truck rolling toward us, very slowly, with hip-hop music blasting out the windows. There was a bunch of young men wearing baseball caps riding in the back. It was crudely painted bright yellow. I couldn't say why, but it worried me.

The pickup truck stopped about fifteen feet from us and four young men climbed out. They all wore sunglasses and there was something vaguely menacing about them.

"*Sasa,*" the man who'd been driving said.

"*Sasa*" means "hello" in the Sheng dialect. Sheng is mostly spoken by young people around Nairobi. It's a mixture of Kiswahili and English and a few tribal languages. I know some words of it because Mukanda likes talking Sheng.

"*Fiti,*" I said, the standard reply in Sheng.

"Don't talk to them," Mama hissed to me. "Get in the car. They're street boys." Street boys. Suddenly I felt very afraid. In Kenya that's what we call criminals.

"Look!" the driver said, smiling broadly as he stepped between us and our car. When he smiled, I could see he had a bunch of gold teeth. "Look, it's Miss Betty and that *manzi*, Lulu. From that show on TV!" *Manzi* is the Sheng word for "girl."

Mama pushed me toward the Land Rover. But now all four of the young men had stepped between us and our car. "Hey, Miss Betty," the young man said, flashing his gold teeth again. "We're just *muenjoyo*. Why you want to leave so *nduthe*?" (*Nduthe* means "fast" and *muenjoyo* means "having some fun," but it didn't seem like fun to Mama and me.)

The young men didn't move. I saw Mama exchange a worried look with Arthur, who started to get out of the back seat of the Land Rover.

"Back in the car, Grandpa!" the young man with the gold teeth said. Arthur seemed frozen. The street boy lifted the tail of his shirt, revealing something stuck into his waistband. It took me a moment to realize that it was the butt of a pistol.

"You get out of my way, young man!" Mama said angrily. I knew she was afraid. But she wasn't showing it now.

Still the street boy didn't move. "Little Lulu," the young man said. "You're a big detective, huh? You gonna be the next Ignatius Sang?"

I frowned. *What was he talking about?* How could he know I was looking into the theft?

For the first time, one of the other street boys spoke. He was smaller than the guy with the gold teeth, but there was something even scarier about him. He didn't move quickly, and his voice was so quiet I almost couldn't hear him. "Let Inspector Sang worry about who stole that sculpture," he said. "It's not your problem."

"*Out of my way*," Mother said. She put her arm protectively around my shoulder. Her hand gripped me so hard that I could feel her nails poking my skin.

"You ever hear the stories about Curious George?" The short man stooped down in front of me so our faces almost met. "Little monkey, always getting in things? Then it ends up in trouble?"

"I don't know what you're talking about," I said.

He made a slow wave of his arm, pointing to

all the shacks around us. "Mathare is a dangerous place. You know what happens to a curious little monkey around here?" He smiled.

I didn't answer.

"*Anadai*," he said in Sheng, "*anadai.*"

The young man stood back up, turned, and strolled toward their yellow pickup truck. The other boys followed, climbing in the back. The driver waved lazily at us, flashed his gold teeth, then drove slowly away. The music thundering out of the windows faded away. Then they were gone.

Mama shoved me into the car. Then she jumped in the driver's seat, and we tore off down the road. Dogs and chickens scattered.

"What did he say?" Mama asked when we'd finally found a paved road again. "Just before they left, I didn't understand what he said."

"He said, '*Anadai,*'" I answered. "It's Sheng."

"What does it mean?"

"'She dies,'" I said. "It means, 'She dies.'"

tisa

After we got home that night, Mama and Baba had a long conversation in another room. Charles and I were specifically told not to come in. But I could hear voices being raised. Mama and Baba rarely argue, so it made me feel really scared.

Finally the door opened and they came out.

Mama said, "Charles, go to your room and do your homework."

"I already did my homework."

"Then go to your room and read."

Charles looked up from his book. "Why can't I read here. I'm just. . . ." Then he saw the grim looks on their faces and he said, "You know what? I think I'm going to go into my room and read."

Mama and Baba watched him go, then they sat down on the couch across from me. They looked at me for a long time in silence. I got this squirmy feeling in my stomach.

Finally Baba spoke. "Your mother and I have discussed this entire situation regarding Mukanda, and here is what we have decided." He put his hands together like he was praying. "First, the fact that you were threatened in Mathare is not accidental. Someone knows about what you're doing, Lulu. Someone who had something to do with the theft of the sculpture. Clearly there's more to this than Mukanda."

"That's what I've been saying all along!" I said. "That's why we need to —"

Baba held up his hand. "I'm not finished."

"But —"

He cut me off. "It seems likely that some kind of criminal gang is behind the theft of this sculpture. Maybe Mukanda is connected to it, maybe not. But the point is, there's someone out there who is very dangerous. And they're going to hurt anybody who tries to expose them."

I swallowed. The nervous feeling in my stomach kept getting worse and worse.

"Your mother and I have discussed this. And we have come to a decision. We absolutely forbid you to continue your little so-called investigation."

So-called? My investigation had clearly exposed something. "But Mukanda —"

"Did you hear me, young lady? You are forbidden. Don't talk about the sculpture. Don't talk about Mukanda. Not to me. Not to your friends. Not to Charles. Not to anybody."

I sat there like a lump, disappointment flooding through me like cold water in my veins.

Mama cut in, "Look, we understand how you feel."

"No, you don't!" I burst into tears.

Mama and Baba looked at each other. "We do," Mama said. "We feel just as helpless as you do. But here's the hard truth. There are bad people in the world. And sometimes you're just not strong enough to fight them."

"This is not right!" The tears were running down my face, down my neck.

"Hold on," Baba said. "We're going to do two things. First, I'm going to go examine Mukanda's mother. If necessary, I'll have her taken to my clinic where I can give her a proper examination."

"And meanwhile, Mukanda's rotting in jail!" I yelled.

"I'm not finished," Baba said. "The last thing is this: We believe that you have discovered something important. There are people whose job it is to investigate crimes."

Just then, there was a knock at the door. Through the front window, I could see a man. He was very tall, with very black skin and a long green coat.

"We've called Ignatius Sang," Baba said. "We want you to tell him everything you've learned."

I nodded.

"But after that," Mama said, "you must leave it in *his* hands."

"Now go get the door," Baba said.

A few minutes later, we were sitting in the garden. Ruth was cooking *pilau*, a dish made from rice and coconut, on the *jiko*. A *jiko* is a sort of portable, pot-bellied cooker. You fill it with charcoal and then cook on the top. Everybody in Kenya has a *jiko*.

"Mmm!" Inspector Sang said as the smell of

coconut wafted over us. "My mother cooked the finest *pilau* in Kenya." He smiled at Ruth. "No offense."

She smiled back. "No, sir. None taken."

The detective took out his pipe, filled it with tobacco, then lit it. The smoke curled up over his head. "Terrible habit," he said, waving at the smoke with his hand. "I started when I was young and stupid, and now I can't seem to quit."

"I can't imagine you were ever stupid," Mama said.

Inspector Sang smiled. He had a nice smile, with a touch of sadness about it. "We all make mistakes," he said. "Even the best of us."

Mama and Baba nodded.

But I didn't. He was really talking to me, I could tell—trying to convince me that Mukanda was guilty. *Oh, she's just a little girl and I'm a big famous police detective. She'll be easy to convince.* That's what he was thinking. I could tell.

Inspector Sang leaned toward me. His eyes were black and piercing, staring straight into my face. "I must tell you, I'm very impressed," he said. "You're quite an investigator."

Now he was buttering me up, trying to make me feel good. And I had to admit, it did feel nice to have a famous detective tell me he was impressed. But I didn't say anything. I just sat there, squeezing my hands between my knees.

"So," he said. "Tell me everything. Not conclusions. Not guesses. Not hunches. Just facts."

I took a deep breath. Then I told him everything I'd found out. I told him about Mr. Abasi's art collection that he kept in a locked room. I told him about my conversation with the curator of the museum who said that Mr. Abasi wanted to buy the sculpture from them. Everything right down to the point where we were threatened by the young men in Mathare.

When I had finished talking, Inspector Sang cleaned out his pipe with a small pocketknife, then tucked the pipe away in the pocket of his shirt. He leaned back and looked up at the sky. Night was beginning to fall. A few stars had begun to peek out of the gathering darkness.

"Let us say, for the sake of argument, that Peter Abasi did this," the detective said finally.

"See?" I said to Mama and Baba.

"Please, wait." Inspector Sang held up his hand. "A detective is like a scientist. The job of the detective is to gather facts. Assemble evidence. Develop a theory. Then test the theory based on those facts. There is no place for emotion."

"Yes, sir," I said.

"So, let's examine the facts. Peter Abasi is an art collector. He keeps all his art in a locked room which only he is allowed to enter. He has expressed interest in the missing sculpture. He was in the studio when it disappeared." He spread his hands. "So, what would you do if you were in my shoes?"

I looked at Mama and Baba. They looked at me expectantly, but said nothing. I looked back at the detective. "I'd open his art room."

Inspector Sang nodded. "So would I." He paused for a long time. "If I could."

"What do you mean?" I said. "You're a detective."

"That doesn't mean I'm allowed to do illegal things. I can't simply force my way into his house. I need a warrant. And to get a warrant for the home of a well-known fellow who rubs elbows with many influential people in this city . . . ?" He shrugged, gave me his sad smile. "Well, we simply don't have enough evidence to justify it."

I stared at him. "That's *it*?" I said. "You're just going to let him go?"

Inspector Sang lowered his eyebrows. "Did I say that?"

"No, but. . . ."

"I am Ignatius Sang," he said. He placed one large hand across his chest. "This is what I do. If Mr. Abasi had anything to do with the disappearance of that sculpture, I'll find out."

Then he stood.

"Don't worry your pretty little head about it. I'll get to the bottom of this."

After he was gone, Mama said, "Are you satisfied now?"

"Yes," I said.

But really? In my heart? I'm not sure if I was.

I went back to my room and lay down on my bed. I tried to sleep, but I just kept staring at the ceiling. The day's events kept coming back to me.

All those women sitting outside the prison, with their bags full of food. Something about it haunted me. They had to wait. We didn't.

Mukanda's mother lying in the tiny little hovel in Mathare. When I got sick, I went to the doctor. She didn't.

Helen, the football player in Mathare. When

I wanted a pair of shoes, I just bought them. She didn't.

And what about Mr. Abasi? He was rich. He was famous. He had important friends. He drove a Mercedes. Was it an accident that Inspector Sang had locked Mukanda up while Mr. Abasi walked around smiling? Maybe, maybe not.

Was it possible that someone like Mr. Abasi could pay a "service fee" to Inspector Sang? And if so, would Inspector Sang look the other way? I just didn't know. There was a big difference between letting a rich thief go free and letting somebody visit a prisoner outside of normal visiting hours, though.

I had a nervous feeling, and the same thoughts kept running around and around in my head. Finally I got up, got my football, and tiptoed through the dark house and out into the backyard. I know it seems crazy, but I just felt like football was the only thing that would make the noise in my head go away.

So I dribbled around our broad, beautiful backyard, with its carefully kept grass. Even though it was very dark, I didn't feel scared. A big wall surrounds the whole house, keeping out all the scary things—and scary people. I tried to be very quiet. I imagined myself blazing past Amos, shooting, scoring. The crowd erupting in cheers.

She shoots! She scores!

I started feeling excited. I dribbled some more, then got ready to take another shot. This time I slammed the ball with all my might. It went high, bounced off the wall, and flew into the alley behind our house. I could hear it bouncing loudly, banging off the roof of our neighbor's garden shed next door.

Baba came running out of the house at the same time as Elias came out of the servants' house. Baba carried a cricket bat and Elias had a machete in his hand.

They stared at me.

"What on earth are you doing?" Baba said finally.

"I'm sorry," I said. "I was just playing."

There was another uncomfortable silence. "Can I go get my ball now?"

Baba frowned. "Elias will go get it. You come to bed now."

kumi

The next day was Saturday, so there was no school. As Ruth poured my cereal and then refilled Baba's steaming cup of tea, I said, "So when do we go, Baba?"

"Go?" he said, looking up from the newspaper.

"You said we'd go and get Mukanda's mother today and take her to the clinic."

Baba cleared his throat. "I said I'd see her. I didn't say I'd do it *today*. I'll try get to it next week."

"She might die by next week."

Baba took off his glasses, wiped them with his handkerchief, then put them back on. "I suppose you'll be badgering me about it all day, won't you?"

"Of course!" I said, smiling.

Baba shook his head, suppressing a smile. "Elias," he called. "I suppose you'd better bring the car around."

* * *

When we pulled up in front of Mukanda's mother's house, a crowd of shoeless children gathered around the car, begging for money. They didn't see cars here very much—much less nice Peugeots like ours. Baba picked up his black medical bag off the seat. I followed him as he pushed through the knot of children. We left Elias to guard the car.

Hearing the noise, Mukanda's cousin, Millicent, came to the door and yelled at the children, who scattered in all directions.

I introduced my father, and Millicent led him inside, where she fussed over him and made him tea and gave him some food. Finally, she stood, pulled back the curtain, and revealed Mukanda's mother. She looked a little better than she had the day before. With difficulty, she sat up. Then she smiled. "You must be Dr. Kibwana," she said. Her voice was so weak I could barely hear her.

Baba turned to Millicent and me, then took out his stethoscope. "If you'd give us a moment," he said. Then he pulled the curtain shut.

We sat in silence as we listened to Baba conduct his examination. Finally he came back out. His face looked stiff and serious. "May I see the medicine she is taking?" Baba asked.

Millicent went to the bare shelves in the tiny kitchen and took down a number of bottles. Baba took the bottles, read the labels, then screwed one open and smelled it. He made a face and shook his head angrily. "I was afraid of this," he said. He set the bottles on the table. "Miss Ngilu," he said, "I'm going to send for a car to drive your aunt to my clinic. I suspect I know what's wrong. But I'll need to conduct further tests before I can be sure."

"Thank you so much, Doctor!" Millicent said.

Baba smiled warmly. "We'll meet you and your aunt at the clinic in an hour or so."

As we went back out to the car, Baba called

for an ambulance. He looked very angry as he sat down in the back of our car.

"What is it?" I asked after he put his cell phone back in his pocket.

He sighed loudly. "The so-called doctor treating Mukanda's mother? He's no more a doctor than you are."

"What do you mean?"

"He's a man who runs a large clinic here in Mathare. He claims to be a doctor, but he's essentially a crook. He sells worthless herbal remedies to people who have no money and nowhere else to go. I've tried to get him shut down many times. But the health ministry says, 'Well, then these people would have no doctors at all. He probably does less harm than good.'"

"But, surely Mukanda could afford to send her to a real doctor."

"I suppose Mukanda took her to him because that's who she was used to. And this. . . crook—he saw that Mukanda had a little more money than most of the people at his clinic. So he figured out just exactly how much money he could squeeze out of Mukanda. And he's been squeezing the poor young man ever since."

"But why didn't. . . ."

"Kenya simply doesn't have enough doctors to go around. Some people get good care, some get bad . . . and some get nothing at all."

"So what's wrong with his mother?"

"I won't know for sure until I do a blood test. But I believe she's diabetic. Her disorder is entirely treatable."

"So you mean. . . ."

"She needs regular injections of insulin. Mukanda could afford to pay for it on his salary. And with enough left over that he wouldn't have to live in this — this miserable wasteland." He waved out the window as we tore through the rutted streets of Mathare.

"Then she'll be okay!" I said.

Baba shrugged. "Not if Mukanda's in jail. If I find out that her problem is diabetes? Well, it will hardly matter. She'll be no better off than she was before."

"Because she won't be able to afford the medicine."

"That's right." He stared glumly out the car window. Soon we were out of Mathare, driving through a better part of Nairobi, where the streets were paved and everyone wore shoes. "Now you see the sort of choices I face every day as a doctor.

Often I know exactly what the problem is. I know that over in Britain or France or the United States there are warehouses piled high with medicines that would cure my patient."

"Why don't they send them here then?" I asked. "Couldn't the companies just donate them or something?"

"Sure. And then they'd have no money and they couldn't make the medicines anymore." We pulled up in front of Baba's clinic, a low building painted white and surrounded by bougainvillea trees. The trees were blooming, their branches ablaze with color.

Mukanda's mother arrived an hour later. The blood test confirmed Baba's suspicions—type 2 diabetes.

Baba gave Mukanda's mother an injection of insulin. "I'm cured!" she said. "You've cured me, Doctor." Mukanda's mother actually stood up and walked slowly across the room toward Baba. She looked twenty years younger than she had just an hour earlier. "Thank you!"

Baba smiled. But I could see by the way he smiled that he was still worried. "It's not a cure," he said. "It's not a cure."

After she was gone, Baba said to me, "Well,

she'll need medicine for the rest of her life. Unless Mukanda gets out of jail, there's really nothing we can do for her."

"Can't we pay for her medicine?"

Baba looked at me for a long time. "Do you realize how many patients like her I see every day? Decent people. Deserving people. If I paid for just half their medicine, you and Charles and your mother would be living in the shack right next door to Mukanda."

"I wouldn't mind!" I said. Though I don't suppose I really meant it.

"Elias tells me your football hit a rake last night," Baba said. "It popped. I can buy you one on the way home."

"Oh," I said.

"If we lived next door to Mukanda?" he said. "That would be the last football you'd ever own in your life."

I didn't say anything.

"We spent thousands of shillings on your football last year. Football jerseys, football shoes, team fees. If you gave all of that up, you could probably buy Mrs. Ngilu enough medicine for the next two months."

I looked at the floor.

"Still want to buy her medicine?" Baba asked gently.

I kept thinking and thinking. I felt like I was in a box that I couldn't get out of. I could almost feel it squeezing in around me. It seemed like I couldn't catch my breath.

"We have to get Mukanda out of jail," I said finally. "We have to prove. . . ."

"That's Inspector Sang's job," Baba said firmly. He pointed to the car. "Look, we've done enough good deeds for today. Let's go and buy you a new football."

kumi na moja

ama! Baba! Watch this!"

I was out in the backyard trying out my new football, showing off my skills to Mama. While I was bouncing the ball off my left foot (137 times in a row!), Mama's cell phone rang. I couldn't hear what she was saying, but I could tell by looking at her face that she wasn't all that happy.

She was just hanging up when I finally dropped the ball. It rolled over to the patio where Mama and Baba were sitting. "Who was that?" Baba was saying to her.

"It was Ruta Garama," Mama said. "He's insisting that he wants to thank me for having him on the show. He wants to give me a piece of art."

"You'd think he'd be angry after his sculpture was stolen," Baba said.

"He seemed oddly unconcerned about that," she said.

"He's bringing it over then?" Baba asked.

"No, that's the thing. He wants *me* to go to *his* studio and pick it out. He was very insistent."

Baba shook his head and laughed. "Artists!" he said. "They act like they're doing you a favor, when all they're really doing is bothering you."

Mama looked at her watch. "I suppose I'd better go get it over with. Will you come?"

Baba cleared his throat and looked around. "Well, uh . . . I've got, uh, some paperwork."

Mama made a face. "That was the weakest excuse I've ever heard in my life."

"Artists make my feet itch!" Baba said.

Mama just shook her head.

I had promised not to investigate anymore. But it couldn't hurt if I just went to visit. And while I visited, I could do a little investigating, right? "I'll come!" I said.

"So Joyce Mehada, the curator at the museum, tells me you wanted the sculpture back," I said to Mr. Garama not long after we got to his studio.

"Indeed! And now I'm doubly upset about its disappearance."

"Do you mind my asking why you wanted it back?"

Mr. Garama blinked, looking at me like I was a little slow in the head. "Because it's mine!"

I nodded. "And do you mind if I ask you what you would do with it?"

The sculptor continued chipping away at a block of wood—his latest piece. "You ask a lot of questions, don't you?"

"I suppose so, yes."

Mr. Garama chipped and chipped, then finally stopped. "What do you think?" he said.

I looked at the huge face he'd been carving. "He looks kind of crazy," I said finally.

He glared at me for a moment. I felt a knot in my stomach. I guess I should have said, "It's really nice," or something like that.

Suddenly Mr. Garama started laughing. "Yes! Exactly. He is crazy, isn't he?" He narrowed his eyes and peered at the sculpture. "You know, a grown-up would have said something pretentious if I'd asked that question. 'You have such masterful command of your medium,' or some ridiculous comment like that. Who cares if I have masterful command of my medium. It's a crazy man!" He stepped back and admired his work with a giant grin on his face. "Yes! Yes! Totally insane!"

His laugh was so infectious that I started

laughing, too. I think Mama even giggled.

He wiped off the chisel with an oily rag, then set it down on a table. "So, my dear," he said. "You're wondering if I stole my own sculpture. That's it, isn't it?"

I felt my face flush.

He slapped me hard on the shoulder. "That's all right. It's a fair question. Let me tell you the whole story."

"Okay," I said. Mama gave me a serious look.

"I made Mau Mau for a competition a long time ago. The government wanted a statue to put in front of Parliament House, something to commemorate our struggle for independence. I won the competition. This was quite early in my career. After it was over, the government said, 'Oh, and by the way, we'd like to exhibit your model in the National Museum.'

"Well, I felt quite honored. So of course, I said that would be fine. They didn't pay me for it. So my understanding was that I had loaned it to them. If I wanted it back, it was mine for the asking."

"Wait, I don't understand," I said. "Is it yours or not?"

Mr. Garama threw up his hands. "Of course, it is mine!" he shouted. "Of course!"

"But Mrs. Mehada said you tried to steal it."

Mr. Garama scowled. "Well, of course, they say that. They claim the government of Kenya owns it, but that's nonsense!"

I rubbed my head. This was a little confusing.

"Apparently, I signed something," Mr. Garama said. "Now the government claims they own it. Me? I say I was hoodwinked."

"But there's this little matter of your stealing it," I said.

Mr. Garama rolled his eyes. "Stealing! That's not what happened at all."

"What *did* happen then?"

"It was like this: A fellow called me and asked if I owned the model for Mau Mau. I said 'Yes.' He said, 'May I buy it?' I said, 'Certainly.' Then I named quite a sizable sum. He said, 'I'll send you the money tomorrow. Have it ready to deliver to me.'" Mr. Garama laughed. "Well, as you can imagine, that put me in a bit of a fix. After all, the sculpture was in the museum."

"So what did you do?"

"I went down to the museum and told Joyce Mehada I was taking it home with me." He frowned. "She acted like she thought I was joking. Then, when I kept insisting, she said that

I couldn't take it. She said it was owned by the museum. She showed me some little piece of paper that I had supposedly signed and then acted as though the matter was closed."

I waited for him to continue, but suddenly he seemed distracted by the figure he'd been carving. He walked around it, eyed it from several angles. "The nose is too big, isn't it?"

I looked at the figure's nose. It was large and hook-shaped. To me it fit his ferocious features just perfectly. "I like it," I said.

He looked at me curiously. "Do you?"

I nodded.

For a moment he seemed irritated. Then he clapped his hands together. "Well then! If you like it, I shall keep it." He seemed to have completely forgotten about his story.

"So what did you do?" I prompted.

"Do?" He looked at me blankly.

"About Mau Mau."

"Oh!" He scowled again. "I did what any self-respecting person would do. I marched straight down to the gallery, tucked the sculpture under my arm, and walked right out the front door."

I started laughing.

"What's so funny?" he asked angrily.

I tried to stifle my laugh. "Well. I don't know. I mean. . ." You can't just walk out of a museum with one of their sculptures. Finally I got control of myself. "Did they stop you?" I asked.

"Did they *stop* me? Oh, my goodness, yes! Alarms went off and people were yelling and pointing and police came running. Next thing I know, I'm lying on the ground with three of the biggest policemen you've ever seen sitting on my back. I was dragged into court and charged with theft. Can you imagine? Me!" He glared at me as though I was one of those policemen.

There was a long, uncomfortable silence.

"What exactly did you expect? That they'd let you walk out with it?" Mama asked.

His glare softened and he sighed. "I don't know, Miss Betty," he said. "When I get mad, I don't think very clearly."

"So did you have to go to jail?"

"No, no, of course not. I told them that all I intended to do was borrow the sculpture and make a cast of it. Then I intended to sell the cast."

"Cast? What's a cast? I thought that was for when you break your arm."

"It's similar, actually. See that thing over there?" He pointed to a large wooden box with red goo running out of the joints. "You put a sculpture in there, then you pour this rubber goo around it. After the goo hardens, you have a big rubber mold. Then you can pour plaster of Paris into the mold. Or even papier machier or plastic. Or you can even press paper inside and then paint the paper to match the sculpture. When you're done, you have an exact duplicate of the sculpture."

I walked over and poked the red goo. It looked wet, but it was actually just soft, flexible rubber.

Mr. Garama continued. "Anyway, I told the judge that I was just borrowing Mau Mau. I said I intended to make a duplicate, then return the sculpture to the museum. Which happens to be the truth. I must have convinced the judge I was just a scatterbrained artist. He dismissed the case."

"You didn't want to keep the sculpture?"

"*Keep it!*" He picked up his chisel and waved it around at his shop. There were sculptures and paintings everywhere. "What do I want with another sculpture?" He studied the piece he'd been working on, then chipped the end off the nose.

"I thought you said you were keeping the big nose," I said.

"I did, didn't I?" He made a funny face. "Oh, well. I'm afraid I've never been much of a

planner. As soon as I make a plan, I forget what it was. Then something else happens entirely."

As soon as he said that, something hit me. There was no way he'd stolen the sculpture from the TV studio. Whoever stole Mau Mau had made a very careful plan. Then they executed it perfectly. They had to shut off the power. They had to use night vision goggles. Then they had to plant them in Mukanda's room—with clown grease paint on them. The whole thing was *way* too complicated for a scatterbrain like Mr. Garama.

Mama appeared in the doorway. "Lulu, we need to go."

"Okay," I said. I started toward the door. Then I thought of something. "You said that the reason you wanted the sculpture back was that someone offered you a lot of money for it."

He nodded. "Yes."

"Do you mind me asking who it was?"

He started chipping from the block of wood, carving the hair around the crazy man's face. "Fellow by the name of Peter Abasi. I'm sure you've seen him before. He announces the news on TV."

I looked at Mama.

"After it was all over," Mr. Garama added, "that fellow Abasi told me he would get that sculpture eventually. 'By hook or by crook,' he said. I remember his words exactly."

kumi na mbili

Every year I dreaded Amos's birthday party. There are some kids you put up with because you like their toys or their house. But Amos? No, Amos wasn't worth it. Every year his parents put on a huge party. There was a band and dancers and a huge cake made in the shape of a lion or a football or something. And every kid who came got to go home with a bag full of expensive toys.

But it just wasn't worth it. It wasn't fun. It was like the whole thing was put on to show you they were important. And you weren't. And on top of that, you had to listen to Amos talk about how great he was. You had to listen to his mother and father talk about how great he was. Kids always cried. Mrs. Abasi always made a scene with one of the servants.

It was terrible, horrible, disgusting, awful.

And it was today. Sunday, right after church.

But this year it was different. This year I was going to prove to Inspector Sang that I was right. This year I was going to get into the secret room.

It was worse than ever this year. There was a huge number 11 (Amos's age) made of flowers and chicken wire propped up in the yard. The band was bigger and louder than ever. Amos was wearing a white suit and a white tie and shiny white shoes. There was a bunch of kids around him. He was handing out sweets from a bag. Kids were crowding around him, sticking out their hands and saying, "Me! Me! Amos, give me some!'"

Amos shouted commands. "Stop shoving! You! Put out your hand! No! Only one!" It was hard to watch.

For the next two hours, there was a parade of games and contests. Servants scurried around after the children, cleaning up spilled ice cream and calming crying kids. More and more people kept arriving, adults as well as children. Everybody brought presents for Amos, until the pile of boxes next to the big number 11 standing in the yard was about as high as Amos.

Eventually, I figured I could get away without anybody noticing. I slipped into the house. Most of the adults were inside, laughing, shaking hands, eating and drinking. I saw lots of my parents' friends there. Mr. Garama was there, talking to Mrs. Mehada, his eyes wide, hands waving in the air. Mrs. Mehada seemed to find him very funny.

I kept moving through the crowd. No one seemed to notice me.

I had two problems. First was finding the art room. Second was opening it. The second problem was not at all minor. But first I had to find out *where* the secret room was. When Mr. Abasi took the painting out the other day, I heard him going down the hallway. But after that, I hadn't paid attention to where he went.

The house was two stories. I decided to try the upstairs first, since that was farthest from the crowd. I found two bathrooms, four bedrooms and a room with a very large television in it. Everything was neat and clean and perfect, like it had come out of a European magazine. It didn't even look like anybody really lived there. I felt nervous and a little guilty for sneaking around their house. Even if I did think Mr. Abasi was an art thief, it still didn't seem right.

But there was no secret room. Or if there was, I couldn't find it.

I went down to the bottom floor. There were people everywhere, so I had to be a little more careful as I walked around trying the handles on the doors. They were all unlocked. I found a room with a billiards table in it, a library, the kitchen, an émpty room full of boxes, a pantry, some closets. But no secret room.

Eventually I found myself in a long hallway in a part of the house where I'd never been before. I checked the first door. It was obviously Mr. Abasi's office. I poked my head inside and looked around. No door to a secret room.

I walked to the next door, twisted the handle slowly and peeked in. At the far end of the room I saw two people arguing. One of them was Joyce Mehada. The other was Peter Abasi. They must have heard the door click, because they suddenly stopped talking and their heads turned toward the door. I shut it quickly, my heart racing. Should I just leave? I stood there without moving. Nothing happened.

At the far end of the hallway was one final door—the only door I hadn't tried yet. I could hear the band outside, thumping away. But still, it seemed very quiet all of a sudden. I decided I just needed to get it over with. If Mr. Abasi had heard me, he would probably have come out already.

I tiptoed slowly down the hallway, my heart thumping in my chest. Just as I reached the door and put my hand on the knob, I heard a noise behind me. I whirled around. It was Mr. Abasi. He looked at me for a long time. "Lulu!" he said finally. There was a big smile on his face, but the smile didn't seem to reach his eyes. "What are you doing?"

"I'm . . ." I blinked. I couldn't think of anything. "I'm . . . " My mind was a blank. I felt my hands shaking and my heart beating wildly.

The sinister Peter Abasi advances on the little girl with a wicked gleam in his red, glowing eyes.

"At last!" he says, "Now I finally have you alone. You have interfered enough in my evil plans!"

He reaches into his jacket and pulls out a long, wicked, curved blade.

"No! Please!" I whimper.

"Too late!" Peter Abasi cackles. "Too late! Now I shall. . . . "

"Are you looking for the bathroom?" Mr. Abasi's voice shook me out of Lulu Land.

"Huh?" I said.

"The bathroom. Are you looking for the bathroom?"

"Oh," I said. "Yes, that's right."

"There's no bathroom down here," he said. "Come with me." He took my hand and led me out of the hallway and down to the bathroom near the living room.

"Thank you," I said.

"Having fun?" he asked, still with the big fake smile.

"Yes, thank you," I said. My mother says that you should be polite to everybody. Even people you don't like.

"Terrific!" He gave me a little pinch on the cheek and stood there looking at me.

I went into the bathroom, closed the door, turned on the water, flushed the toilet, then peeked out. Mr. Abasi had disappeared into the crowd of guests.

I quickly went back to the quiet hallway. It was still empty. I walked to the far end. Every footstep seemed as loud as a gunshot. I kept waiting for Mr. Abasi to appear again, knowing that if he saw me here again, he'd realize I wasn't looking for the bathroom. Would he suspect what was really going on?

I got to the far end of the hallway, put my hand on the knob and turned it. The knob rotated slowly,

with a loud, metallic creak. I was so nervous! I could feel sweat beading up on my forehead. I looked over my shoulder. The coast was still clear.

When the knob stopped turning, I pushed the door open and stepped inside. I found myself in a large, wood-paneled room. There was a cabinet full of hunting rifles at one end of the room. On the wall hung the stuffed heads of zebras and wildebeest and a big, ugly, beady-eyed warthog with curved yellow tusks sticking out of its mouth. A stuffed hyena crouched at the far end of the room, mouth wide, teeth bared. It looked almost like it was ready to spring across the room and bite my head off.

I closed the door softly. It was only then that I noticed—to my horror—that I wasn't alone.

A boy was sprawled on a large leather couch. Amos! His eyes were wet and red-rimmed. He was looking up at me, wide-eyed. He pawed at his face, wiping away what were obviously tears.

"What are *you* doing here?" he asked.

I shrugged. Now I was cooked. I was sure he'd go running off to tattle on me to his mother and father. But he didn't. He just sat there looking at me. He didn't look like Amos the Big Jerk. He looked like a sad little kid.

"What's wrong?" I asked.

He didn't say anything. He just shrugged.

I don't know why I cared. But he looked so pitiful that I couldn't help it. I went over and sat on the couch next to him.

Finally he sighed loudly. "I hate it!" he said. His voice was soft, but full of anger.

"Hate what?"

He spread his arms wide, as though taking in the whole house, the party, his family, everything.

"What's the problem?" I asked.

"My parents don't care about me. To them, I'm just like a new car. Something to show off to their friends. If I'm not the best football player, the best student, the handsomest boy, the best dressed, then they don't care about me." He shook his head. "I mean, this whole party—I don't want all this junk. I'd just like to have a few kids over and eat some cake and play football."

"You mean this wasn't all your idea?"

He frowned at me. "Of course not! What do I need a bunch of dancers for? I *hate* dancing! And that big number 11 in the yard, with all the flowers on it? Flowers are for girls!"

"I don't really like flowers all that much myself," I said.

"And all these kids?" he said. "I don't even know half of them. And the ones I do know are mostly obnoxious."

"Thanks a lot!" I said.

"I don't mean you," he said. He hesitated for a moment. "Actually, I wish there was only *one* person at the party."

"Who's that?"

He stared at his white shoes, but didn't answer.

"Nelson Kirimi? Winston Atema? Luke Tawa?" I named all the most popular boys at our school.

He shook his head.

"Who then?"

He seemed embarrassed suddenly, squirming around in the chair.

"*Who?*" I demanded. I liked the idea of embarrassing him.

He kept looking at the floor. Finally he muttered, "You."

I stared at him. "Me!"

He kept looking at his shoes.

"I thought you hated me," I said. "You're always mean to me."

He shrugged. "That's 'cause I like you."

"You're mean to me because you like me?" That didn't make any sense to me at all. But then, as Mama always says, "Boys are not like you and me. Their brains are backwards."

"I'm sorry," he said in a small voice. "It seems like I'm always being mean to people. Especially people I like."

"That's dumb," I said. "Why would you be mean to people you like?"

"It's scary, I guess," he said. "What if they don't like you back?"

What do you say to a thing like that?

Outside the music suddenly stopped. A voice came over the loud speaker system that the band had been using.

"Amos!" It was his mother's voice. "Amos! Paging the handsomest, smartest, best football player in the world! Amos! Where are you? Come outside so we can cut the cake!"

"I guess you better go, huh?" I said.

Amos crossed his arms and pushed out his lower lip. "I'd rather stay here and talk to you," he said.

"They'll just come and find you," I said. Which meant they'd find me, too. Which meant I probably wouldn't be able to sneak around the house anymore. Which meant I wouldn't find the missing sculpture. Which meant Mukanda would stay in jail. Which meant. . . .

"No," he said. "I'm not going."

"What are you going to do? Hide under the couch or something?"

Suddenly he seemed excited. He grinned and jumped up off the couch.

"Want to see something cool?" he asked.

kumi na tatu

Amos walked across the room. There was a high shelf of books lining the entire wall—old leather-bound books.

"Amos!" Amos's mother's voice came out of the PA system again. "Amos! Come immediately. Everyone is waiting on you."

Amos ignored her. He stopped in front of the bookshelf and ran his finger across the spines of the books. "I'm looking for *The Man-Eaters of Tsavo* by Lt. Col. H. W. Patterson. It's a book about lion hunting."

"*Lion hunting?*" I said, walking over to the bookshelf. I didn't see what was so cool about lion hunting.

"Oh! Here it is." He looked over his shoulder nervously. Then he leaned toward me and whispered. "My father has a secret room."

My eyes widened. "You know where it is?"

He frowned. "How did you know about it?"

"He, uh, mentioned it the other night while you were playing video games."

Amos smiled. Still in a whisper he said, "He pretends that you have to open it with a key. But you don't."

"Then how do you get in?"

"I snuck in here one time and learned the secret!"

With that, Amos hooked his finger in the top of the book and pulled the top forward, until it stuck out about five centimeters. For a moment, nothing happened. "Wait," Amos said, holding his finger to his lips.

I waited. It seemed like the moment stretched on endlessly. But then there was a sharp click. Followed by a deep grinding noise. And then the entire bookshelf slowly swung open!

"Amoooooossss!" His mother's voice cut through the air. Coming out of the speakers, she sounded like some kind of robot. "Amos, where are youuuuuuuuuu?"

"Let's go!" Amos said. He grabbed my hand and pulled me through the door into a musty-smelling dark space.

There was another click and the door began grinding shut. The sliver of light coming through the door grew smaller and smaller and smaller.

And then we were in total darkness. Suddenly it was completely quiet. Quiet as a tomb. (Not that I've ever actually *been* in a tomb. But I imagine a tomb would be this quiet.) We couldn't hear Amos's mother. We couldn't hear the murmur of guests. We couldn't hear music.

My heart leapt. The secret room! We were in the secret room!

"Lulu Rehema Kibwana, may I present his Extremely Huge Honorableness, the Prime Minister of Kenya."

Ignatius Sang and I stand in a giant marble hall. In front of us are hundreds of really important-looking people wearing tuxedos or black evening gowns. They all stare expectantly at us.

The Prime Minister is a large man with a broad face. He sits on a sort of throne and wears a purple silk sash across his chest that says "Prime Minister" in gold letters. As Sang speaks my name, he bows in my direction.

The Prime Minister rises to shake my hand. "It is my deepest honor and pleasure, young madam."

I curtsy, holding the edges of my beautiful silk dress with my fingertips. "No, your honorableness, it is my deepest honor and pleasure."

The Prime Minister turns to the audience and says, "Ladies and gentlemen, I wish at this time to recognize the courage, the fortitude, the extremely big smartness of this young lady. Exclusively because of the efforts of Lulu Rehema Kibwana, the national police have arrested a notorious ring of art thieves. Were it not for this young personage, even that master of detectiveness, Ignatius Sang, would have been unable to crack the case."

The audience bursts into applause. The people are clapping and clapping. I see that Mukanda is among them, wearing a beautiful white suit. His face is beaming and he is clapping hardest of all.

Finally the Prime Minister raises his hands to quiet them. He reaches into his pocket and pulls out a large, ornate medal, sparkling with diamonds and rubies.

"Lulu Rehema Kibwana, it is now my pleasure to confer upon you with the highest honor of the Kenyan nation."

"Sometimes the lights take awhile," Amos whispered, yanking me back from Lulu Land.

All I could hear was my heart beating and my pulse rushing in my ears. Oh, and also I could hear Amos breathing, his face very close to mine.

There was a snapping sound from the ceiling, then two long fluorescent light bulbs flickered on. We looked around the room. There were large metal shelves full of paintings in the middle of the room. Big paintings, little paintings, watercolors, oil paintings.

Amos walked over to a shelf and began looking through the paintings. "Wonder if he's got any pictures of football players here. That would be cool."

On any other day I might have been interested in paintings of footballers, too. But all I cared about was the Mau Mau sculpture.

I scanned the room with anticipation. *Where is it? Where is the man with the spear?*

But there were no sculptures in the little room. None at all.

"Hey, check this out!" Amos said. "Look at this old guy's face. He's got his eyes all squooshed shut like he's farting."

All of my excitement began to drain away. "Is this *it*?" I asked.

Amos looked around. It seemed to be dawning

on him that a room full of art was actually not all that fascinating. "Well, there's a bunch of money in a cigar box. And there's a chest with my father's army uniform in it."

That was not what I had in mind. At the far end of the room, behind all the shelves, was a tall wooden crate. It was the perfect size for a sculpture. "Wait a minute, wait a minute!" I said, pointing. "What's in there?"

Amos shrugged. "I don't know." He didn't seem interested.

"Let's look," I said.

"Don't you want to see the old guy farting?"

"Maybe in a minute." I hurried over to the tall crate. There was a latch on the side. And in the latch was a lock.

"It's locked," I said, a wave of disappointment sweeping through me. What if I got this far, only to be defeated by a combination lock? I was sure the sculpture was in there. But I had to be able to prove it.

I smacked the side of the crate with my hand. It was solid as a rock. There was no way to get into that box. Not without the lock being opened.

Amos came up beside me. "Maybe there's a mummy inside!" he said.

"Maybe."

"Sometimes they put the combination on the back of the lock," he said. He flipped the lock up. There was a tiny white sticker with some numbers on the back. He spun the dial and the lock popped open.

I gave him a hug. "Amos, you are the greatest!" I said.

He looked startled. I guess he wondered why I cared so much about some junky wooden box. Then he grinned. "I know," he said. He swung the door open. We peered into the crate. It was crammed with some kind of straw packing material. I scrabbled furiously through the straw, throwing handfuls of it on the floor.

Inside was a sculpture.

A sculpture, yes. But it was the *wrong* sculpture.

My heart sank.

It was just one of those old tribal carvings like they had in the National Museum. It was a man with big googly eyes and a straw skirt and his tongue sticking out.

Amos giggled. "Same to you, you goofy blockhead!" He said to the sculpture. Then he stuck his tongue out. Then he started laughing.

It would have been funny at any other moment. But just then? When I'd expected to solve the mystery and clear Mukanda's name? It was like in those cartoons where the piano falls out of a tall building right on top of your head. I just felt squashed flat.

Amos kept sticking his tongue out at the sculpture, then laughing, then sticking his tongue out. Finally he noticed I wasn't laughing.

"What?" he said defensively.

I just stood there. Not only was there going to be no medal from the Prime Minister, it was clear that I'd been wrong the whole time. It wasn't Mr. Abasi. It never had been. Someone else stole the Mau Mau sculpture.

Finally, I stooped over, picked up the packing material and started jamming it back in the box. I felt like an idiot. Why had I ever suspected Mr. Abasi? He was stuck-up and bragged too much, but that didn't mean he was a thief. All the grown-ups were right. I was just a silly kid, trying to pretend I was an investigator. It was just another Lulu Land fantasy. I was never going to play in the women's World Cup finals. I was never going to be the best football player in Kenya.

And I was probably never going to solve this

mystery. Who knows, maybe Mukanda did it after all.

"We'd better go," I said, my voice coming out dull and tired.

Amos looked around the room again. When we first came in, it had seemed almost magical. Now it just seemed bare and ugly, like the back room of some little shop.

"Yeah," he said. "I guess we'd better."

"Where *were* you, you naughty boy?"

When Amos came out onto the stage where the band had been playing, his mother grabbed him and hugged him. He stood there like a rag doll, arms limp. Nothing moved but his eyes. He looked at me for a long moment. Then he rolled his eyes.

I laughed. Maybe Amos wasn't so bad after all.

kumi na nne

*L*et's review the facts," said Inspector Sang.

"Okay," I said. I was at my house, but the Inspector wasn't really there. I was just pretending he was there so that I could try thinking the way he thought; maybe then I could figure this out.

"The power went out at 4:27," I imagined him saying. "That's only three minutes before the end of the show. At the end of the show, the doors of the studio were sealed and the police arrived. We searched the premises. We didn't find it. The statue weighs fifty-three pounds and stands three feet high. Too large to have been hidden in a drawer or a filing cabinet. So it must have been taken out of the studio in that three-minute period, correct?

"And the power was only out for twenty seconds or so. Not long enough for someone to have run out of the building and back. That means someone in the room took it, gave it to an accomplice, and returned to their place in the room. The accomplice must have then taken it out of the building. Probably through the back door and into the parking lot. Does my logic make sense?"

"Yes sir." This was working!

"Good. So who was in the room? Five children who were on the cast of the show. Could they have taken it?"

"No, it was too heavy."

"Correct. That leaves six adults: Peter Abasi, your mother, Ruta Garama, the museum curator Joyce Mehada, Mukanda, and the cameraman Arthur Kamau. Now, Joyce Mehada had polio when she was a little girl and has walked on crutches ever since. She couldn't have carried the statue. Arthur was holding the camera and was connected to a variety of cables and wires. So he couldn't have carried it either. So we're left with Peter Abasi, your mother, the sculptor, and the clown.

"Of those, three are prominent people with longstanding reputations in the community. One is a young, strong, athletic man with a criminal record, connections to street boys, and financial difficulties. Now, of those four people, on whom would you focus your attention? The facts lead to a suspect."

"I just don't think he would have done it," I said to myself. I was beginning to think that Sang might be right. Trying to think like he did was helping me, but it was also making me sad.

I slid into the computer a DVD of the show when the statue was stolen.

A menu came up with a list of the cameras. There were two cameras used to shoot the show. This DVD had the footage from both cameras on it.

I started watching. Most of it was just boring stuff. It showed Ruta Garama getting out of the car. The next shot showed a worker from the museum unloading the crate that contained the sculpture. Joyce Mehada and Mr. Garama were supervising. Then there was a shot of me and the other kids shaking hands with Mr. Garama.

Then there was a long stretch where the camera seemed to have been left on by accident inside the studio. It showed the worker from the museum, accompanied by Mrs. Mehada. The worker opened the crate, then lifted the heavy statue onto the pedestal in the middle of the studio. Mrs. Mehada directed how she wanted it placed.

The man left the studio, presumably to return to the truck. I remembered that he hadn't been in the studio. Mama had specifically mentioned to Mrs. Mehada that she didn't want too many extra people in the studio during the broadcast. For a moment there was no one in the studio but Mrs. Mehada. She looked around the room as if she was examining how the light fell on the statue. Then she reached out and adjusted its position a bit, pushing the statue to one side. After that she hobbled to the door on her crutches. The camera continued to run. There was a sound of footsteps, and then the camera cut to another scene.

I frowned. Something odd had just happened. But I couldn't put my finger on what it was. I backed up the video and watched the scene again.

"Oh my gosh!" I said. "Mama! Baba! Come here!" I pictured Sang watching me with interest.

Mama and Baba ran into the room. "What's wrong?" Mama said.

"Watch this," I said. Suddenly I thought of something. "You know what? Never mind."

Mama looked at me with a curious expression. "All that shouting . . . for *nothing*?"

"Well," I said. "I was wondering if I could do another story for *KenyaKidz*?"

"What story is that?"

"This thing with the sculpture. It's gotten me interested in museums. What if I did a segment about Joyce Mehada?"

Mama looked at Baba. Then at me. "You want to do a story for the show? About Joyce Mehada?"

I nodded.

She shrugged. "Okay."

She started to leave.

"And . . .uh . . . could we shoot it tomorrow?"

Later that afternoon, when I was sure nobody could overhear me, I picked up the phone. My hands were trembling as I dialed.

"Hello," a man said.

"Inspector Sang?" I said. "It's Lulu Kibwana."

kumi na tano

It was four o'clock the next day. Mama had driven me to the station to pick up the camera. Then we had driven to the museum.

I set up the camera in Mrs. Mehada's office. It was aimed at her across her desk so that you could see a computer screen behind her. She had a very nice office with artwork hanging on the walls. I was trying to act normal. But I didn't feel normal. I was scared and nervous. But a little excited, too.

"Oh, Mama," I said. "I forgot the tape for the video camera. Could you get it from the car?"

"I suppose I could," Mama said and she left.

"Before I ask you questions on camera," I said, turning back to Mrs. Mehada, "I'd like to do what we call a pre-interview. I'll just talk to you for a few minutes. That way I'll know what to ask you once we turn on the camera."

"Of course." Mrs. Mehada smiled at me.

I asked her a few dumb questions about her job. Then I said, "So about the crutches you use?"

"I had polio when I was a child," she said.

"Would it be hard for you to lift a sculpture?"

She cocked her head and looked at me curiously. "Quite impossible," she said.

"Do you mind putting this in your computer?" I said, handing her a DVD.

She looked puzzled. "Okay."

After a moment a video image popped up on the screen. It showed Mrs. Mehada in the studio. She was standing in front of the Mau Mau sculpture. She looked around, then reached out and adjusted its position.

Mrs. Mehada swivelled around, her face suddenly going hard. "What is this?"

"No one stole the sculpture from the studio," I said.

Mrs. Mehada's eyes narrowed. "I don't understand what you're talking about."

"I had an interesting conversation with Mr. Garama a few days ago," I said. "He told me that you could make a rubber mold of a sculpture. And then use that mold to make a perfect copy."

"I wouldn't know anything about that."

"I think you would. You told me you studied

sculpture with him. He told me you could make the copy out of anything. Foam rubber, plaster. Even paper. You could paint it and it would look just as solid as if it was made of stone."

"I think our interview is over," she said.

"No, not yet," I said. "I think you paid the man who moved that sculpture into the studio to pretend he was carrying something heavy, when in fact, it was made of paper. Then, when your helper turned off the power, you grabbed the sculpture, wadded it up, and put it in your bag."

"Ridiculous."

"The proof is on the video," I said. "You lifted the sculpture with one hand and moved it."

Mrs. Mehada stared at me for a long time. I could see a vein throbbing in her temple. "It was an optical illusion."

"You think Inspector Sang will believe that when I show it to him?"

The museum curator's eyes narrowed. "What do you want, little girl? You want something or you would have gone to him already."

It was strange, but I wasn't nervous anymore. I was mad. I was mad because this lady had tried to ruin somebody's life. Somebody who had done nothing wrong to her. "You framed Mukanda. I want you to promise to return the sculpture and figure out a way to prove Mukanda didn't do it."

Mrs. Mehada swallowed. When she spoke, her voice was thin and quiet. "Not possible."

"Then I'll go to Inspector Sang."

She glanced toward the door, as though expecting Mama to burst through any time.

"Tell me why you did it," I said.

Her shoulders slumped. "My brother-in-law is the warden of the jail, so he knows a lot of street boys. He told me about a man who wanted to sell stolen art. He said I could make a lot of money without any risk. The man would pay me to look at some art and tell him if it was authentic." She shook her head sadly. "It was a lot of money. I said 'okay.' Next thing I knew, he was blackmailing me to do other things. Then one day he came to me and said, 'I have someone who wants to buy the Mau Mau sculpture. Figure out a way to get it for me.' "

She looked at the floor for awhile.

"I told him it was impossible," she said. "We have too much security here. But he said he would turn me in to the police if I didn't find a way to steal it. What could I do? Then I was talking to Ruta, and he told me about the show. I realized it was the perfect thing. I could get the sculpture out of the museum and switch it in the truck for a fake made of paper. Then, poof, in the middle of the show, it would disappear."

"And what about Mukanda?"

"We had to find somebody," she said bleakly. "He was the perfect suspect. Everybody else in the room was beyond reproach. All I had to do was plant the night vision goggles in his office. I put a little red grease paint on them to seal it."

"So Mukanda had nothing to do with it." I said. "He's totally innocent."

She nodded, then took a deep breath. I could see she was starting to regain her composure.

"Who have you told?" she asked.

"Nobody," I said.

"*Really?*" I could see her thinking. Did she still have a chance to get away with it?

"And did you make a copy of this?"

I blinked, like she'd caught me off guard.

She smiled suddenly and popped the DVD out of the drawer. "Well, then," she said. "I hate to say it, but now it's just your word against mine. A little girl against a respected art curator." She laughed. Then she snapped the disc between her hands. It shattered, bright shards of plastic flying through the air. "Your word against mine," she said.

There was a brief silence. Then I smiled. "Actually, not," I said. I pointed at the video camera. "The little red light that usually comes on when a camera is running? It's broken. I've been taping you all this time."

Mrs. Mehada stood up sharply, grabbed her crutches, and hobbled toward me. For someone on crutches, she was pretty fast.

I flinched and tried to get away.

"You horrible little girl!" she shouted. She raised her crutch as if to hit me with it.

The door burst open and Inspector Sang walked in. "I don't think so, my dear," he said. "If you don't mind, Mrs. Mehada, please sit down. I need to place you under arrest."

kumi na sita

I never really believed in Lulu Land. I mean, when I'm daydreaming, it seems real. But as soon as I stop, it all fades away.

But this time, it became real. I really was on the front page of the newspaper. The prime minister really did shake my hand. Then Inspector Sang made me an honorary Detective Inspector, First Class, in the Kenya Police. I didn't get a medal, and there weren't any people in tuxedos and evening gowns watching, and it wasn't in a big marble hall. It was just in a little office in a government building. But still . . . *Detective Inspector, First Class*! That's a pretty big deal.

My Mama and Baba came. My best friend came. Even Amos came. I seem to be playing football with him a lot these days. He still sulks when he loses. But that's okay. Nobody's perfect.

Oh, I forgot to mention Mukanda.

He's back on the show. His mother's doing really well, and he's moved to a decent house in a safer, nicer part of Nairobi.

Before every show, he gives me a hug and whispers, "Keep dreaming, Lulu. Dreams are real!"

And he's still the funniest clown in the world.

Wasn't it shocking to find out who really stole the statue? I bet some of the things you found out about Kenya were surprising, too. I decided to show you pages of my journal (usually I keep it private) to share a little more about my life and my brilliant country...

FOOTBALL IS MY LIFE!

(Isn't it weird how Americans call it soccer?) I made the team at school and get to play usually as striker or 2nd striker because I'm fast, fast, fast like a cheetah! Am I bragging too much? What if one day I could meet my hero, Kenya's great female "football star" Maisha Adhiambo? I can't believe some people still think football is just for boys. One day I'll play professionally and become a famous athlete like Maisha.

I think people imagine Kenya being a big hot savannah because we're right on the equator. But our weather is perfect because of the altitude, over 4,000 feet up! You can only shoot animals with a camera (hooray) because Kenya's government outlawed the hunting of wild animals in 1977 to preserve our natural heritage.

Can you believe these pictures are BOTH taken in Nairobi?
In 2005 they counted 5 million people – some very rich but most
so poor they desperately try to survive on about $1 a day. We have
high rises, nice shopping malls, high tech this and that. But we also
have the Mathare area which is very, very poor. It has no drinking
water, electricity or trash disposal. It just makes me sad every time
I think of it. But I'm happy when I go visit with Baba to help the
sick people there because we can make a difference.

"To celebrate the birth of Lulu, let's explore the Cradle of Humanity!" was how mama announced the big plan for my 11th birthday. They call it "the cradle" because lots of people think human life began there. The valley is huge (3,500 miles) with part of it running right down the middle of Kenya. Confession: even though it was cool to learn how volcanoes created the valley during dinosaur times, the best thing was when my favorite of all animals, a giraffe, came so close to the Land Rover he licked the window!!!!!!! Very slimy. (I love journals, you can say anything!!!)

How to speak Kiswahili:

Jambo (JAM-boh) = hello

asante (a-sant-EH) = thank you

Rafiki (ra-FEE-kee) = friend

twiga (TWEE-ga) = giraffe

The Masai tribe is so so famous probably because they camp near the preserves and make such beautiful beaded jewelry. We do have about 40 different tribes in Kenya! I'm glad to be Kikuyu because Masai girls often have their marriages arranged by their fathers even before they're born. And when they stay in one place (they're mostly nomadic) they live in kraals, huts the women make out of cow dung.

At my school, Parklands Academy, there are about 300 kids ages 6 -12. We get there at 8:00 a.m. and stay for 8 hours. In between: Math (very hard), Geography (love it), English (hard), Swahili (fun), FRENCH (love, love, love it) and History (o.k.). We wear uniforms, but I'm not complaining. More than 3,000,000 primary kids in Kenya don't get to go to school at all. Last week on a school trip to a museum, we saw this mask that I thought was so pretty.

It's hard to know what to believe sometimes.
Some people are so superstitious. I try not to be,
but I follow these (just in case).

#1. Never say 'goodbye' at night – the person you
say goodbye to might die.

#2. Always eat fish from the head towards the tail.
I don't know why but you better do it.

#3. Beware, whatever you do on New Year's Day,
will be repeated all year through! Like if you cry,
you will cry the whole year.

#4. An itchy right palm means that you will
receive money.

When I was little we went to the Masai Mara Reserve.
To get there took so long, 5 hours from our house.
It's the most popular park in Kenya because it has so
many lions. But you can see lots of elephants, rhinos and
hippos there too.

Everyone got excited because a lioness was hunting
down a tiny gazelle. I couldn't look when

she caught it, though.

Sometimes things that are unfair bother me even if they were really long ago. In 1930, even though our country had over 30 million people, over HALF our farmland was reserved for just 2,000 white settlers – mostly British. It was so unjust that finally the native Kenyans rose up and fought for independence. We won our freedom in the Mau Mau Rebellion. (Remember the Mau Mau warrior statue?) I'm always proud that members of my Kikuyu tribe played an important part in creating the first modern government of Kenya. A Kikuyu was even the very first president!

Today my friend Caroline and I were lazy all day just imagining the places we'd go when we grow up. Don't worry dear parents, after University. First stop is Paris for me to show off my French, watch wonderful football, see the sites. Caroline will study film making in America, which is brilliant. But we'd never live anywhere but Kenya – we both want to do everything we can to make it a better place to live for EVERYONE.

<u>What Lulu loves as far as food goes:</u>

I love pizza! Thank goodness there are so many kinds of food from all over the world in Nairobi. I love nyama choma (roasted meat like goat). I wish we had it every day instead of just on special occasions. I love chai tea (tea with milk and sugar) in the morning served with warm mandaazi, a sweet deep fried dough cake (like a doughnut). Excuse me while I go get some.

I don't love ugali (sorry mama!) – Too bad cornmeal mush is Kenya's national food. But if mama bakes it into bread, it's delicious with salty butter!